FOLK LORE, OLD CUSTOMS
AND SUPERSTITIONS
IN SHAKESPEARE LAND.

I0615183

BY

J. HARVEY BLOOM, M.A., Hon. F.S.G.

Author of *Shakespeare's Garden, The Griffins of Dingley,
English Seals,* etc.

FOREWORD.

THERE are a number of small and beautiful villages, hidden away among the blue hills and glorious valleys of the Cotswolds, where until lately the placid peace of the countryside remained quite undisturbed by the restlessness of modern life, wherein men and women lived as their forefathers had done for centuries, or very nearly so. In these places, and in hamlets far distant from the beaten track, old myths were handed down, old manners held their own, and the folk kept folk-faith ; they were all but self sufficing.

The old church was a centre, the ancient manor house a place of warm affection, and they thoroughly understood one another, leading a simple unambitious life, with its cares and sorrows, its very real joys and pleasures. Among these villages I had the good fortune to have many humble friends, and from them learnt what their grandparents had handed down of the old customs of their vill.

Enclosure acts have played havoc with the past, but in one of these hamlets, Crimscot, the act has never been put into operation, and the strips and ridges of the common field remain to-day as they have ever been. In this district lived my old friend Mr. F. S. Potter with his aged sister, almost a centenarian ; their old-world garden served them as a place to make friends with bird and butterfly. There, feeding the nuthatches, hearkening to the hoot of the owl, the two lived in peace with the world *and made peace*, for in their presence all the discontent and quarrels of life were soothed away. No word of unkind condemnation ever passed their lips, they lived as peace makers and were loved.

They gave me of their store, wise observation, boundless knowledge. I promised that when I could it should be published, with such small additions as I collected, in order to record ere it was too late the passing of the ancient ways of hand workmanship, the personal relation of master and man, before the paid agitator had his way. Their memory recalled the practices of a century. Whether it was worth the while those who deign to read must say. Much is not new, very far from it, but I hope some little has been added to the knowledge of folk-lorists.

Notes alone would hardly suffice to piece themselves together, so it seemed needful to put down some elements of the law and the general trend of history, and thereby form a more or less connected story. This little book is not primarily meant for those who know, but for those to whom Brand and Fraser are sealed books. It may serve to show workers in other counties that there is a good deal still left worthy of record in the small happenings that left their impress on the village mind.

My thanks are due to all who helped me. They are too numerous to mention by name, but I thank them none the less.

Little has been said of the village church and its clergy, not because they have no part in the life of the village, but because they deserve a different treatment. As in other things they changed with the times, but never,

I think, did either the priest or the church he served be other than an influence for good in the daily life of the place. Nor was the hunting parson of the eighteenth century less watchful over his people according to his lights than his Anglo-Catholic successor.

The little book is not exhaustive, and its readers may easily be led to condemn its arrangement, but I trust its shortcomings will be forgiven. All of us have much that needs forgiveness, most of all an author.

J. H. B.

December, 1929.

CONTENTS.

AUTHORITIES CITED.

A. M. S. Mrs. A. Savage, Stratford-upon-Avon. MS.

Brand, John (ed. Sir Henry Ellis). Observations on the Popular Antiquities of Great Britain. Bohn's Ant. Lib. 1854. 3 vols. 8vo.

Cardwell, E. Synodalia. Oxford, 1842. 2 vols. 8vo.

E. D. D. Wright's English Dialect Dictionary.

E. S. Mr. Edmund Smith. MS.

F. G. S. Mr. Fred. G. Savage of Stratford-upon-Avon. MS.

Fitzherbert, Sir Anthony. The Boke of Husbandry, 1534.

Fraser, Sir J. G. The Golden Bough. 12 vols., 1907—15, 8vo.

F. S. P. Mr. Frederick Scarlett Potter of Halford. MS.

Hales. M. R. Amphlett, John, Halesowen Manor Rolls. Worcester Hist. Soc. 2 vols. 4to.

Hone, William. The Year-Book of Daily Recreation and Information. London, 1832. 8vo.

J. S. Mr. James Simms. MS.

Laneham, Robert. A letter whearin part of the Entertainment vnto the Queens Maiesty at Killingworth Castl in Warwichsheir in the Soomerz Progress in 1575 is signified. 1575. 16mo.

Maitland. The History of English Law. Sir Fred. Pollock and Fred. Will. Maitland. Cambridge, 1898. 2 vols. royal 8vo.

P.R.O. Public Record Office.

FOLK LORE, OLD CUSTOMS AND SUPERSTITIONS IN SHAKESPEARE LAND.

CHAPTER I.

THE FARMER AND HIS MEN.

When William of Normandy broke the "shield wall" at Senlac, and Harold fell, the Normans found in England a ruling aristocracy, the Eorles, thegns, ceorls and theows, respectively the upper ten, the middle classes and the lower five of the period. The survivals in custom, tradition and song, which are so rapidly disappearing from our midst, have reached us across the centuries from the homestead of the ceorl, or the cot of his slave, and these people themselves inherited them from yet earlier traditions, going back in some instances to the very dawn of the Aryan invasion, at least to the people of the new Stone Age if no further.

The Normans wrought some changes, old things were called by new names. The Norman Count and Baron ousted the Saxon Eorl and thegn from their rights and land, and the free ceorl and socmen the unfree villain, cottar, and bordar of Domesday and beyond. The theow very shortly disappeared; his masters did not understand a man who had no rights, and had no particular use for him. He gradually rose in the world, gained certain rights, was no longer a mere chattel, and even at rare intervals owned property of a humble kind.

The villain farmer, who became either a freeholder by a rise in the world, or smaller until he was reduced to a grade but little superior to the cottar, was the prototype of the tenant farmer of to-day. He differed from the Saxon ceorl in that he was obliged to have some lord—someone, that is, who could be responsible for his good

B

behaviour and could be made to bear the blame, or at any rate pay a money fine, if his conduct was unsatisfactory. To this lord he took an oath of fealty and became, as the phrase ran, " his man "; another phrase states that " he went with his land to his lord." In other words, he gave his freedom and placed his means of livelihood under his master's protection. His land was still his own, and he paid no rent for it. The lord obtained a stalwart retainer, who would fight for him without any enquiry into the merit of the case. The lord saw to it that his follower was not ejected, was not unduly oppressed, and had enough food and sufficient instruments of husbandry to do his work in a practical and proper manner. To the freeholder he was not so bound.

Very shortly his possession became assured by deed, and he and his wife and children secured from being turned adrift by a mere whim, so long as their services were strictly rendered, and such services were settled according to the custom of their own particular manor. On the death of the father the eldest son steps into his place, pays the succession duty (the heriot), and his son in due course follows him. There were moreover other means of enriching the villain. He might hire land through some specified service such as training hounds, tending hawks, making deer hayes, or even by teaching the lord's daughters fancy-work. The ordinary villain, however, held his lands by servile service. He must plough and sow, reap and harrow, tend the swine, mend the deer hayes, gather fuel and nuts so many days in the week, with extra service in haytime and harvest, such as mowing, carrying corn, etc. By these means the lord was enabled to get most of his work done without the payment of wages; and his man was provided with land and a home and the means of furnishing his cottage and stocking his holding. In theory, at the owner's death, all returned to the lord, in which case the heir would have been penniless. In practice the lord took a single thing, the dead man's best animal. On the payment of this heriot the son was admitted to the father's holding, which he cultivated exactly as his father had done, and without any inclination or indeed small possibility of making improvements.

Nevertheless they were very far from being free agents. They could not on any account leave their lord and go away to someone else ; they could only marry their sons and daughters with their lord's consent. They could not carry corn to be ground except to their lord's mill, nor might they have a sheep-fold of their own. The villains had to barter away some of their freedom for the protection of a powerful master, who found their services useful and convenient. Each little homestead was at this period almost entirely self-supporting. All, or nearly all, the food, meat and drink, the clothing and appliances were raised on the farm itself, or at the most in the village. Indeed there was practically no money in circulation for the buying and selling of goods, and before town life began and burgess holdings generally established, there were very few traders. Most of the needs of the community were easily met by an exchange. The blacksmiths did their iron work in return for assistance in ploughing and harvesting. The carpenter wrought in like manner, and even the parson was paid for his spiritual services in similar fashion. When dispute arose, the jury of the manor heard the cause and settled it in accordance with their customs, which were inviolable, and equally binding on master and man.

We have spoken so far of the villain. The lower orders differed merely in degree ; they had less land, less pretentious dwellings, rougher work and rougher fare, but on the other hand had less binding services or rather less responsible ones. All of them had a cot, household goods, and sufficiency to support their family. Paupers there could hardly be, and in the early middle ages few if any could have suffered seriously from want, except such free men as for some cause or other had fallen into destitution.

The records of great ecclesiastical owners teach us that in Warwickshire the classes or society ran much as follows. In the manor of old Stratford in 1252 we find knights, free tenants, customary tenants and cotmanni ; whilst in the neighbouring estate of Worcester Priory at Alveston, there are only freemen and villani. It is very interesting to note that a large number of the inhabitants had good Saxon names. The knights held their land by military service ; the freemen paid rent, and a rate, shall we call it, in lieu of castle guard. The customary tenants paid rent and also rendered services ; they sowed, ploughed, harrowed and reaped, carted hay and corn, and paid various tolls for ale, if brewed to sell, also for leave to turn their hogs out for pannage ; they paid tithe to the church, and hundred silver to the Crown. Their unfreedom was marked by the payment of a heriot, and they might not send their sons off the manor, nor marry their daughters without their lord's leave. Their weekly services had been commuted for an annual rent of eight shillings for the messuage and virgate of land, which form the normal tenement of each.

At Alveston in like manner they perform much the same services ; each ploughs a quarter of an acre in winter, each harrows it at Martinmas ; they help at hay-making, pay aids and market toll ; each man works for three days weekly unless he is on boon work, which consists of hoeing, lifting and carrying, while he goes to help the lord's harvesting with two men.

Villeinage was abolished in England in 1381. By that date ancient custom and tradition had been rendered inoperative by the Black Death. The visitations comprised under this generic term altered entirely the whole system of farming. It was no longer carried on under the lord's bailiff, but taken over by a class of yeomen, who worked the land assisted mainly by their family. The older system, owing to the scarcity of labour and consequent high wages, could no longer pay its way. The new men were provided with stock, seed and what capital they needed, and after a trial of half a century the newer mode became generally established ; but more than one attempt had been previously made to enforce the older regime.

The Statute of Labourers* ordered that every man, whether bond or free, should serve any master who might require his services, who was not allowed to pay him more than ordinary wages, living meed or salary. His own lord had first claim upon him and his services, but might not employ more men than he needed. If he ran away without reasonable cause he could be imprisoned. This was followed by the statute of 1352, by which it was enacted that ploughmen, drivers of the plough, the shepherd, swineherds, deies (that is day-labourers) and all other servants are to serve at the old wages, and be hired by the year and not by day. They were ordered to bring openly to merchant towns their instruments of labour, and there to be hired in a common place and not by a privy. This is the origin of the " Mop," or hiring fair, which takes place in Stratford-on-Avon, Shipston-on-Stour and elsewhere, though it is now many years since farm servants were hired at them, and indeed farm servants in the old sense are all but extinct.

As we have already noted, the yeoman farmed his land largely by the help of his sons and daughters, assisted by his hired dependents, and such a farm was almost entirely self-supporting. The young men and maidens lived wholesome if hard lives, and intermarried with others of their status. The husbandman only differed in degree ; he held less land, had less capital, and less means of ever becoming the possessor of his holding. As a rule he held by copy of court roll, and his tenure was often secured for the life of himself, his wife and children.

The day-labourer and the higher grades, such as shepherds and swineherds, gradually ceased to have land of their own, and were almost entirely dependent upon their wages.

* Close Roll, 23 Edw. III., p. i., m. 8d.

CHAPTER II.

FAMILY LIFE : MARRIAGE.

It will be convenient to commence our description of the family with some account of the marriage law of the church and manor, and of the traditional ceremonies observed : more especially as such matters are but little understood at the present time, and the origin of our modern observances are for the most part unknown.

We are so accustomed to look upon marriage on the one hand as a solemn sacrament, or on the other as a purely civil rite, that medieval practice comes to us as a shock. It is so very contrary to all we have been led to expect. Our most learned exponents of ancient English law tell us that no religious service was necessary, nor was the presence of a priest by any means an essential. A marriage took place anywhere at any time, since it consisted of a mutual vow to take one another for man and wife. It needed no record and no witness. It was the easiest possible thing to wed, but a very difficult thing to prove. These difficulties led in time to the civil power ordering espousals to take place at the church door, since that was recognized as the most public place in the village, just as to this very day all legal notices are affixed to it, although the village post-office or garage would be far likelier to serve the purpose.

In 1254 a case occurred in the law courts which illustrates the foregoing remarks. A certain tenant of the Crown died holding his land in chief, and a jury was duly summoned to hold the usual enquiry as to who might be his heir. They declared that this tenant, William de Cardunville, had espoused a lady named Alice at the church door, that the pair lived together as man and wife for sixteen years, and had four children, one of whom (Richard) was four years old at his father's death.

Then there came another woman, who stated that she

had a son named Richard by the same William, and that she could claim him as her husband on the strength of an affidavit made between them. It is true that they had lived together but one year, but the church allowed her plea, and the verdict was given in favour of a marriage that was in no way solemnized.

A religious service held at the church door had very strong merits when there was any doubt as to the legitimacy of the children. The marriage was a public one, and there were witnesses. It was good so far as a lay jury were concerned, and only in the church courts was it likely to be set aside for a previous contract.

Nevertheless, the exchange of a few words in private sufficed to make the parties legally man and wife ; in fact, to avoid concupiscence the canonists made marriage absurdly easy, and then multiplied impediments to make a valid marriage extremely difficult to prove.

Under the system of villeinage the lord of a manor would suffer severely if any of his villeins left the land. He would have one less to till it, and the same applied to the women folk, hence no man holding by servile tenure could marry without his lord's consent, or allow his daughters to do so. On the other hand, the lord might not compel a girl to marry a man she disliked, though he need not approve of the man she chose. In practice a small fine secured liberty ; at other times the seneschal of the bishop, the cellarer of the priory, or the representative of the lord would make a suggestion, usually a fair one no doubt, but one that was almost an order, and was expected to be obeyed.

It was at Halesowen in 1274 one John de Romesle was offered a certain widow in marriage, and accepts without hesitation ; yet on the same date one Nicholas de Kewak does not so readily obey—he asks leave to put the matter off for awhile until he has spoken with the cellarer.* In any case most freeholders were fined, and paid merchet on the marriage of their daughters, but a few were so free that they were able to carry out the

* Hales. M. R., f. 55.

Gilbertian procedure of paying merchet to themselves.*
This was by a clause in the Magna Carta ; no woman
can be made to marry against her will, but if she wishes
to do so, she must fall into line with the rest, and
procure the requisite permission.

If we turn from legal points and difficulties to immemorial traditions we find ourselves on very interesting
ground, and a much varied one.   Traces are not wanting
in English tradition of marriage by capture, whilst
marriage by purchase was general.   The purchaser having
paid the price agreed upon, the bride became his property,
though not as a slave, since her rights were duly guarded.
The rhyme in which the medieval espousals are expressed
retains ample trace of such a marriage—

> With this rynge I thee wed,
> And this golde and silver I thee geve,
> And with my body I thee worshippe,
> And with all my worldely cathel I thee endowe.

Both the bride-sale and the use of the ring were known
to the Romans, and existed among our Saxon forefathers ; a sale pure and simple became a covenant with
the bride's kin, to secure for her the morning-gift if she
chose her lord's will.

There is some dispute about the actual moments of
the married state : did it or did it not begin with the
betrothal ?   This important prelude took place between
the bridegroom and the bride's legal protector, and in
some respects was a form of marriage covenant, and in
others resembled our engagement.   An action, for what
we should call breach of promise, could be brought by
either against a third party, whether on the man or
woman's side, and if the bridegroom failed to keep the
betrothal, he forfeited the bride-price ; if the bride failed,
he not only kept his money, but could recover from the
parents or guardians of the bride a third more.

Espousals, although very important, could be set
aside, as we have seen, but not without serious harm

* Hales. M. R., p. 3.

done to one or other party; but by the twelfth century the canonists invented a form which could not be annulled. If a boy and girl solemnly declared that they do take one another for man and wife then and there, it was considered a valid marriage, and binding for all time, even if the pair did not hereafter live with one another; on the other hand, if they said "would" in place of "do," circumstances might easily arise when such a betrothal could be set aside.

"Of all people in the world, lovers are the least likely to distinguish precisely between the present and future tenses; in the middle ages, marriages or what looked like marriages, were exceedingly insecure."[*]

The church service consists first of the ancient espousals, then of the Benediction of the married, which, as it stands, is imperfect, since the wedding Mass is wanting to complete it. For this reason the canon law forbade the marriage ceremony after noon, as after that hour no mass could be said. At this mass the bride and bridegroom received the holy mysteries veiled, a custom in itself dating back to those yet earlier times, when the canon of the mass was said within the drawn curtains of the sanctuary.

Its survival is still seen in the wedding veil of the modern society wedding, but these veils were not within the reach of the country folk, but even so, they provided "falls" of linen in their bonnets.

It must not be forgotten that a prejudice exists against a long engagement—

Happy is the wooing
That's not long adoing,

but it does not always follow that the other extreme is wise. Among Warwickshire folk a hasty, or at any rate irregular, marriage is spoken of as "a marriage over the broomstick." My informant (Mrs. T. M.), who is perfectly trustworthy, told her mother that she was weary of service and wanted to be married. Her mother's

[*] Maitland and Pollock, *Hist. Engl. Law.*

reply was this : " If you want to be married you must
jump the broomstick." The jumping consisted of holding
the broomstick horizontally behind the jumper and, without letting go, jump backwards over it—a difficult task.
In this case it was not accomplished, and the lady had to
wait.   This ceremony was in use, or is said to have been
in use, among gypsies, and has been recorded as peculiar
to them.

    As has been suggested above, the church was long in
obtaining control of marriage. It was not, however,
until the year 1200 that the then Archbishop, John Peck-
ham, ordered the publication of banns three several times
prior to marriage.   Even so, marriages without banns or
askings were solemnized and accounted good and lawful.
The presence of a priest was not made binding until the
Council of Trent issued a decree to that effect.   Under
the rule of Cromwell marriage was considered a merely
civil rite ; banns were published on three several market
days in the market-place of the nearest town, and the
ceremony took place before a justice of the peace.   There
were, however, exceptions ; banns were sometimes asked in
church, and a clergyman not infrequently officiated.

    After the church obtained due control the espousals
consisted of six essentials.   The first, a verbal expression of
free consent uttered from earliest times in the vernacular
and in rhyme ; the second, the offering of spousalia or
espousal gifts, which became in time ceremonial, the
bridegroom placing a few gold and silver coins on the
priest's book.   The third was the giving and receiving
of a ring, a rite as we have seen practised by the Romans,
and used doubtless as a symbol of possession.   The ring
was blessed by the priest and sprinkled with holy water,
to eject the evil spirit that might be within it.   Rings
were of gold and silver or of brass, not necessarily plain,
but often chased and wrought into ornaments.   They
were generally inscribed on the inner surface with posies,
such as—

          God above, increase our love—

    or,   As God decreed, so we agreed.

The presentation was accompanied by a bunch of flowers, of which the elaborate wedding bouquet is the modern form. In case a ring was not forthcoming, either from poverty or forgetfulness, the church-door key served as substitute, or at need a curtain-ring sufficed. Indeed, "marriage by curtain-ring" is a phrase which in our country expressed a hasty wedding. Much virtue was attached to a wedding ring; it was used as a charm in many infant complaints, and its accidental loss was very seriously taken.

It does not seem to have been customary among the peasantry to give engagement rings. They came to church together and sang out of one book, but this cannot be a very old custom in itself.

The fourth rite was that of the kiss of peace, which was usually given by means of a pax, but there is no doubt that in comparatively recent times in some parts of England the priest was expected to kiss the bride after the ceremony and before the wedding-party had left the church. In Warwickshire, and doubtless elsewhere, this portion of the wedding was in more recent times carried out by the best man.

The fourth ceremony, that of joining hands, is an example of a simple action conveying with it actual possession, or, as the lawyers would term it, seisin. The bride and bridegroom became possessed of their mutual bridal rights in one another, as husband and wife, by this action, just as a man purchasing property took possession by taking a spade in his hand and digging up a spit of turf.

The sixth, the settlement of a dowry on a bride (in writing), was a later interpretation of the agreement made by the representatives of the young pair before espousals; this was needed lest by accident the bride and her future offspring might be penniless.

The oldest account we have of midland wedding customs is found in the burlesque performance given by the earl of Leicester, in his castle of Kenilworth, to amuse Queen Elizabeth. It is due to one Laneham that the details have come down to us, and, in spite of its coarse buffoonery, it throws important light on customs which have only descended as starved survivals.

The bridegroom wore his father's tawdry worsted jacket, and a fayr straw hat with a capitall crown steeple-wyze, and a pair of harvest gloves as a sign of good husbandrie. The bryde was led between "two ancient parishioners" and was attended by a dozen damsels for bridesmaids, three of whom carried special cakes before the bride, while a deformed lout bore the "bride-cup," "of a sweet sucket barrell a faire turned foot set thro it, all seemly sylvered and parcel gylt, adorned with a beautiful braunch of broom, gayly beguilded, for rose-mary, from which two brode brydelaces of red and gold buckerram hung fluttering in the air. The wedding-guests moreover had every wight, viz., the buckeram bridelace upon a branch of green broom (canz rosemary is scant there) and bridelaces to match tied on the left arm 'for a' that syde lyez the heart.'"

One can trace the "something borrowed, some-thing blue" that must be worn. In the blue wedding ribbons, of Heaven's own colour, there may well be some relic of Sun-worship, although usually con-sidered to be a sign of fidelity. It is true we have changed to white as an allusion to the innocence and purity of the bride. It is difficult to see why broom was made the substitute for rosemary, which, as Shakespeare reminds us, was "for remembrance" and enters rather largely into the menage of our ancestors.

The loving-cup and the spiced ale are no new features either. Of course it is no longer possible for even a mad bridegroom to "drink up the muscatel and throw the sops in the sexton's face"; nor is it a modern custom to drink a loving-cup in church, or eat the bride-cake there; but all these things are still practised outside. We have a hot-house button-hole in lieu of rosemary, white rosettes in lieu of blue buckram, and champagne or ale as the case may be instead of muscatel.

The loving-cup has but recently gone. Vessels were

made for the purpose with three handles, and inscribed with the words, " Hand that to me, my dear," and these were hawked round the villages for such occasions. The writer has had examples described to him and the mode of procedure mentioned. The loving-cup was first filled and offered to the bride, who however was at once requested by the bridegroom to hand it on to him ; the formula was identical with the inscription on the vessel. There was no indecent allusion of any sort, it was merely a more modern version of Laneham's " well sucket barrell."

For the spiced cake we have our sugared bridecake adorned as of old, not, it is true, with gilded broom, but with sugar flowers. The wights and damsels are still with us.

The village wedding group of old tradition consisted of four persons—the bride and bridegroom, the bride-groom's man and the bridesmaid. The ordinary dress of the groom would be a well-worked wedding-smock, gaiters and a beaver hat. The patterns worked upon the smock in linen thread were locally distinct and handed down from mother to daughter. This smock was worked by the bride, and the buttons were hand-made, or very rarely of brass. The bride would wear a serviceable dress of soft grey or white, with a bonnet to match, trimmed with jasmine and artificial orange blossom. Her dress to be correct must have—

> Something old, something new,
> Something borrowed and something blue.

It must be remembered that blue is the colour of the Blessed Virgin Mary, as Queen of Heaven, and that in tradition she took the place of Juno as patroness of married women. Nor must the bride be completely dressed before the moment to start for church—at the very last instant a stitch must be added to prevent ill-luck ; nor, according to Laneham, must she look at herself in a mirror before she is dressed, nor after her toilet is completed, otherwise ill-luck will follow.

The colour of the gown worn by a bride should be either white, blue or pink—

> Married in white, you have chosen all right,
> Married in green, ashamed to be seen,
> Married in grey, you will go far away,
> Married in red, you will wish yourself dead,
> Married in blue, love ever true,
> Married in yellow, you're ashamed of your fellow,
> Married in black, you will wish yourself back,
> Married in pink, of you he'll aye think.

Of these colours, green was worn at times as a sign of incontinency ; red, as the colour of fire, is a devil's colour ; blue has been referred to above ; black is the emblem of mourning, and if worn foreboded an early death to one of the contracting parties ; yellow was accounted the colour of jealousy. Black was adjudged much as an accidental encounter with a funeral procession, which, on the way to or from the church, was in like manner reckoned a harbinger of early decease.

In choosing a husband it was advisable not to marry a man whose surname began with the same letter as the bride's—

> To change the name, and not the letter,
> Is a change for the worse, and not the better.

A doctrine that perhaps can be traced to some instinct against the marriage with relations—a possibility far more likely to occur in early days, when men and women rarely strayed from their native spot.

Another warning is announced as follows :—

> Who marries between the sickle and the scythe
> Will never thrive.

This may have originated from the restriction placed by the church. Weddings were practically forbidden between Advent Sunday and the Octave of the Epiphany, and from Septuagesima Sunday until the Octave of Easter ; also from Rogation Sunday till Trinity Sunday.* But behind this was the older Aryan idea of the winter's

---

* Cardwell, *Synod.*, p. 134.

gloom. Marriages were only suitable when all nature was bursting into song, and the sun held supreme power.

Apart from the ceremonies at church are those carried on on leaving the church and at home. The curious idea that by throwing something such as an old shoe, or in later days rice or confetti, meaning that it is possible to throw good luck to the happy pair, is perhaps very primitive, or at any rate accords well enough with the current of early thought, making a simple figurative action convey a real thing.

It was considered lucky for the bride to be driven to church horsed with grey horses, or even to meet animals upon the way of that colour. Edward Savage suggests that this idea may be the origin of the general practice of " using greys."

As we have seen, the bride cake and the bride ale is no longer consumed in church but at the house. The knife must be inserted in the cake by the bride—she must offer the sacrifice—but it must be cut up by the brides-maid, or in some districts by the bride's mother. The cake must not be entirely consumed, a portion must be preserved to keep the groom faithful, and to bring good luck. This reserved portion was often eaten at the christening feast of their first-born, a pledge and tie of fidelity being then possessed by the pair in their child. The girl friends of the bride usually retained a portion of their cake to place under the pillow on which they slept, in the hope that in their dreams the form of their future husband would appear. Its potency was increased if passed through a wedding ring.

If by any chance a younger sister was married before an elder, the elder was ordered to dance in her socks at the wedding, or in a pig trough, as a sign of shame in her failure to make herself sufficiently agreeable to secure a husband before her younger sister. The country weddings in the forties of the last century still held it customary to scatter flowers both wild and cultivated before the bride and bridegroom on their return from church. In one instance reported from Charlecot the churchyard pales were decked with flowers and evergreens, the latter were frequently intermingled with the flowers cast before the happy pair. In another instance rose petals were strewn.

At Whitchurch in the hamlet of Whimpstone it is now usual to fire a gun as the wedding party come back from the church as a sign of joy, but the practice is of no antiquity.

It is considered unlucky if the bride and bridegroom return to the house at which the wedding festivities have been celebrated before they reach the place for which they have set out ; this is probably only a specialized form of that ill-luck which awaits any person setting out on a journey and returning before it is accomplished.

CHAPTER III.

CHRISTENING AND BIRTH CUSTOMS.

In medieval times there seems to have been considerable fear that a new-born babe might be exchanged for a stranger's, or even that fairies might replace the newly-born child with one of their own weakly elves, and the child would then grow up sickly and troublesome. It was believed that such an exchange could not take place after baptism.

It was probably largely due to this idea that the bedroom of the mother was crowded with her friends and neighbours, a proceeding not uncommonly fatal to the sufferer. The study of any old parish register will show at once that mortality at birth was very high, and the service of thanksgiving for safe delivery was therefore a very real mark of gratitude to God.

In the villages very few would have the advantage of a qualified medical man ; the forthcoming generation were practically left to the care of the village midwives, very often half witch and half herbalist. Their knowledge was profound as far as the tradition of their calling went, and the medical man of the period was not much more efficient. Still-born children were common, and had not the families been exceedingly large the rustic of even the seventeenth century would have had few sons and daughters to carry on the family name. Still-born children are sometimes entered in the parish register as a " creature of God," or " a creature of Christ," in place of the more usual expression. They were interred in the churchyard by the parish clerk, as a rule in the evening.

If a pregnant woman met a hare, she must stop and make three rents in her shift, or the child would be hare-shorn, _i.e._, would have a hare lip ; this is yet another instance of the part played by the hare in Warwickshire folk-lore.*

* Langford quoted by E. S., see Br. iii. 202, who quotes Home's _Dæmono-logie of_ 1650.

Occasionally a baby came into the world partly covered by a caul—if the face were covered it was called a mask ; such an accident was accounted a sign of luck. In the usual way the caul was burnt and used as a mode of divination, the number of future children being foretold by the number of " bosts " made while undergoing consumption.   If the child possessed a " mask " at birth it was considered certain that he was secure against death from drowning, and the mere possession of the " mask " was almost as effective.   Mariners did much to obtain and carry with them such a safeguard, and when obtained it was most carefully preserved.

At Stratford-on-Avon it was feared that if the mask were lost the child would go abroad, but if retained they were assured that it would stay at home in England. In Birmingham a dried caul is said to be effective if carried on the body against rheumatism.

The new-born child must be carried downstairs as soon as it is washed, but here and there (though not generally practised) it was considered better to take it up a step or two, or even to mount a chair, lest its chance of rising in life should be jeopardised.

As soon as possible after birth a little butter or honey, or, in later days, butter and moist sugar were placed in the baby's mouth, not merely for its sweetness, or even to " clear its throat," but because honey had many rare virtues attributed to it, whence its name " Treacle of Heaven."

The women of the past centuries were stronger physically than those of the early Victorian period. They led simple, active and contented lives in their own homes, with little nervous excitement and probably a small amount of worry, and as one of the consequences their period of lying-in was of less duration than in modern practice.   Cases are not unknown of women busy at work again next day, or on the same day as the confinement ; but there was usually a period of from four days to a fortnight spent in the bed-chamber.   In primitive times, and among a very primitive people women after child-birth were taboo and not allowed to see the sun for twenty-one to a hundred days.*

The custom of seclusion of the mother is probably due to this, at any rate in part, a religious or superstitious custom underlying most practices even in this twentieth century.

During this period a special form of nourishment called "caudle" was taken by the patient, and it was part of the duty of the Squire's lady, where there was one, to provide this from her kitchen. The liquid consisted of old ale and oatmeal mingled with sugar and spices, and was fetched as a rule by the husband. If either a tendency to imbibe or undue curiosity led him astray, it might well chance that the caudle was consumed on the journey home and the patient went without, the inducement of old ale probably overcoming distaste for oatmeal with which it was mixed. Caudle wells exist in many places, and were possibly used when old ale in sufficiency was not forthcoming. There was such a spring at Crimscott in Warwickshire, and others at Shottery and Snitterfield, and also at Long Compton. The Moggles well at Cherington is said to have been used for a like purpose.

It is still considered unlucky to allow a child to see itself in a looking-glass, but such a superstition can hardly be of any great antiquity, since looking-glasses were too unusual in a cottage or farm in early days, unless their rarity and the suspicion always accorded to unknown articles gave rise to the idea ; or another origin might have been that the custom was transferred from a pool of water to glass.

If the new-born infant seemed restless and made a sucking movement with its lips, it was supposed to show a desire for something its mother had not been able to supply. In Warwickshire this something took the form of hare's brains reduced to a jelly. It was an ordinary custom on the Alscot estate to send a deputation to the

---

* Fraser, *Golden Bough*, i. 19.

lady of the manor to beg a hare's head for the purpose; this custom was kept up to the last thirty years. There is also an Ilmington record which carries us back more than a century. It will be noticed that the hare figures largely in Warwickshire folk-lore, and was one of the totems of the Kelts. It is thus very likely that the custom referred to is of great antiquity.

CHAPTER IV.

BAPTISMAL LORE.

The day of the week on which the infant first saw light indicated good or bad luck as to its future. The following rhymes bear witness to the belief which ultimately goes back to the influence of the planet ruling the natal day :—

> Monday's child is fair of face,
> Tuesday's child is full of grace ;
> Wednesday's child is full of woe,
> Thursday's child has far to go ;
> Friday's child is loving and giving,
> Saturday's child must work for his living.
> A child born on a Sunday is born to be a lady or a
> gentleman.
> A child born on Christmas Day will be wise and good.

Or this version :—

> Sunday's child is full of grace,
> Monday's child is fair of face ;
> Tuesday's child is full of woe,
> Wednesday's child has far to go ;
> Thursday's child is inclined to be thieving,
> Friday's child is free in giving,
> Saturday's child works hard for his living.
> A child born on Christmas Day will have the power of
> seeing spirits.

The act of choosing the child's name was not quite so difficult then as now. The number of christian names was far more limited, and the difficulties of choice were yet further reduced when but one christian name was needed, and the fanciful ideas borrowed from modern novels had not come into vogue. In the time of our Saxon forefathers surnames did not exist and titles were rare. On the other hand, christian names having to do duty as surnames also were extremely varied, but even this variety proved insufficient for its purpose. Surnames came very gradually into use, at first merely adjuncts to the christian name, taken from the place of habitation, the trade, or some peculiarity of the owner.   In this way good folk of whom we write would by the fourteenth century be distinguished much as follows : John-by-the-way would have a brother William-atte-the-lane-end and a sister Margaret-atte-the-welle.   In the nearest town they might have relations known as John the black, or Robert the poulterer, or William le Witesmith, and so on, while Robert le rudde, John the little, or Thomas the smith would be sufficient distinction.   From such names more modern forms have sprung.

For christian names we are dependent chiefly on those familiar to us in the Bible and such Norman-French and Saxon names as have retained favour, while a host of fanciful appellations, some times in no sense suitable, came into fashion in the nineteenth century.

In practice it was customary to name the eldest son after its father or grandfather, and the eldest girl after her mother, while the rest of the family were in like manner named after some benefactor or aunt or uncle. It was very general to choose godparents of the same name, and during the reign of Mary and some short distance into that of Elizabeth godparents' names were entered in the parish register with that of the child.

Register entries are not strictly speaking original documents.   They were supposed to be written up at the Easter vestry, when the churchwardens made up their return to the Bishop; as a result the two very frequently differ considerably, not only in spelling, but in the omission and addition of entries.

In cases of foundlings a name was given by the churchwardens ; as an example, in the register of Shipston-on-Stour there is entered the baptism of a small mite labelled Peter Churchporch, because he was found in the church porch on St. Peter's Day.

Baptism was usually administered at an early date and the form of total immersion was observed probably throughout the Middle Ages.   Salt was placed in the

child's mouth, with the words "Receive the salt of wis-
dom, that God may be gracious unto thee, into life
everlasting. Amen." A taper was held in the water, it
was thrice breathed on, and both it and the child
anointed with oil. The infant was invested with a
chrisom with the words, "Receive a white and spotless
vesture, which thou shalt wear before the Judgment seat
of our Lord Jesus Christ, that thou mayest have life
eternal, and live for ever and ever. Amen." All these
ceremonies were omitted from the English service in
1552, although the entries of burial of chrisom children
are not infrequent long afterwards.

Godparents were formerly called Gossips, and parents
were not allowed to act in this capacity until 1865 ; no
more than two were formerly customary, and never more
than three. The present custom dates back to the Synod
of Worcester in 1240, but was probably far from generally obeyed.

In cases of danger children were baptized at home,
and even midwives could perform the ceremony, but
there was always much opposition to lay baptism, and the
priest was as a rule fetched. It was formerly the custom
even among the poor for the gossips to give the child a
spoon, with the handle worked into the statuette of one
of the apostles, but gifts do not seem general nowadays.

It is still considered unlucky if the child does not cry
during the baptismal service, but the writer has not heard
that it is a sign of early death.* It would be resented if
a male child were christened after a female one. Country
folk still speak of privately baptized children as half-
baptized, and they are not considered christened until
publicly received into the church.

In the country the baptismal service forms part of the
regular evensong of the day, which is usually Sunday,
unless the child be a bastard, in which case the service
takes place before the congregation have assembled. This
is happily dying out.

* Br. ii. 78.

It is still customary to have a christening cake and a small feast, but in memory of even middle-aged inhabitants of Whitchurch this was a more serious affair and the principal dish was stuffed chine ; beer, as usual on such occasions, was consumed in large quantities, for the village folk all brewed at home and still do so, and very strong beer it is.

The late custom of putting off baptism for a month or more after birth renders it possible for the mother to attend, but formerly it was general that her churching should take place after the christening ; indeed she usually returned the chrisom to the Minister when she came to be churched. It would be considered a very wrong act to go out of her house for any ordinary business before she had been to church. There seems to be no traces surviving of any churching feast, though such a feast must have been general.

This may be as good an opportunity as any to mention an instrument formerly common to every cottage, but which is nowadays never seen. The machine has gone, but evidences of its presence remain. In many old cottages a dowel hole may be seen in the beam of the flooring directly above it, with another in the floor beneath it. In these holes a short pole was placed so that it might freely turn at will, and at a convenient height a short arm projected, to which was attached a pair of leather thongs ; these were tied about the waist of a toddling infant and the child learnt to find its feet. Supported by the shorter pole it made a series of more or less circular journeys, much in the manner of a tethered donkey and with far less freedom, but at the same time was secure from harm while its mother attended to her household work. This contrivance was called a swing. Some of the older cottages at Whitchurch preserve its memory.

CHAPTER V.

CHILDREN'S COMPLAINTS.

Some fifty years since, a farmer's wife in Ilmington was advised by a gypsy woman to roll her child naked in the first snow which fell after its birth. It was, she said, their custom to do so to make the infant strong. A similar custom is recorded by A. M. S., but in this case the feet only were placed in the snow as it ensured immunity from chilblains. Rubbing chilblains with snow is well known and probably effective. Another cure of even less pleasant character was commonly practised. The feet or hands were dipped in urine before going to bed, and tales are current among village folk of servants doing this and being unable to extricate their foot from the "member mug" without the fracture of that article.

The berries of the Bitter-sweet (*Solanum dulcamara*) were used, well rubbed in ; they were preserved in bottles for winter use. The custom of beating the affected part with holly sprigs is not unknown in the county, and was probably general.

"White mouth" in recent times is treated with borax and honey, but in former days a yellow frog held by the hind legs and placed in the child's mouth for suction was the cure used at Hunscot, the idea being that the disease was consumed by the frog. So in 1707 a live frog held in the hands was seriously considered to take away fever.

Croup was usually treated by giving the patient goose oil as an emetic, and a supply was kept in most farm-houses. If the child died, it was not attributed to the failure of the oil to effect a cure, but that it had not been applied soon enough.

Teething, with its attendant convulsions, was rendered harmless by a necklace, and such necklaces were worn because they were supposed to give some mysterious protection to the wearer. In some cases the twining stems of Traveller's Joy (*Clematis vitalba*) were in request ; a case recently occurred at Stratford, when the grandfather, learning that the child was in convulsions, said that he would soon cure her with a ring of this plant.   In Whitchurch, Halfwood (*Lycium chinense*) was used, the stems being cut into short lengths and threaded in the manner of the old-fashioned jet bugles.   At Broad Marston in Gloucestershire short lengths of elder threaded on a string were worn, but the elder must come from plants seeded by birds in the pollard tops of willows and must be cut by the father at full moon.   In other cases a red thread or red ribbon was worn.   At Southam nine strands of red sewing silk were twisted together round the child's neck, and the loose ends caught together on the breast. In Lancashire the granddaughter of a midwife told me her grandmother made them with knots at equal distances, one inch apart, and put them on the new-born baby as soon as it was washed.   The necklace was never removed until teething was safely over.   In like manner the children of Shottery wear bead necklaces as a preventive of sore throat, but among the very poor a single bead suffices.   It is considered most unlucky to break the string and lose the beads.

To the present day a " coral " is much in request among babies.   It was supposed to preserve the wearer from the malicious practices of witches, and it helped to " Breed and sett faste the teeth "*   Orris root, in which there was no medical virtue, took its place to some extent, but has died out within the memory of the writer ; possibly the modern " pacifier " abomination has supplanted it.

The first teeth of children, whether falling out naturally, or removed, should be sprinkled with salt and burned, since if by chance a dog ate one, the child's new tooth would be a dog's tooth (E. S. quoting Langford, but adding :) " Many people observed the rule of salting and burning their second teeth if they came out, but not, as far as I know, as a preventive of ill-luck,

* Br. ii. 85.

but as a survival of the infantile practice after the reason for it had been lost. A milk-tooth, after it had dropped out, should be placed in a mouse's hole, for then the new tooth would be as small as that of a mouse's. It was considered very unlucky to weigh a baby or cut its nails before it was twelve months old. If this was done it would never grow strong and well; the prejudice still exists, and district nurses are looked upon with scant favour for bringing ill-luck on the infant. The nails, if cut, make the child light-fingered; they should be bitten, not cut.

Whooping-cough, called locally chin-cough, had certain peculiar treatment. The patient was passed through the cleft of a split tree, usually an ash. The tree, having been split with a chisel, was wedged apart, and the child drawn through; the tree was then allowed to close, either naturally or by being nailed together. The life of the sufferer was then supposed to coincide with the life of the tree. Such a tree grew on the edge of Shirley Heath in Solihull, and is quoted by Brand from the *Gentleman's Magazine* for Oct. 1804,* with other instances in the same neighbourhood, but in these the malady of the children was rupture; but the efficacy of a split tree for rickets, rupture or whooping-cough was widely believed in. Grose, quoted by Brand, says that a young ash must be selected and split for about five feet, the fissure must be held open, and the child stripped naked, passed three times through it, head foremost; the tree was then bound together with pack thread, and as the bark healed the child recovered.†

Of somewhat similar nature is the cure by a moocher, or rooting bramble, which had bent down and taken root —the child was passed three times through this natural arch. This cure is known in West Norfolk, so is probably of wide diffusion. Another whooping-cough cure in North Warwickshire consists of making the patient swallow a roasted mouse; in the southern section of the county it was given to children who were unable

* Br. iii. 289. † *Ibid.*, 287.

to pass the night without wetting the bed. It was given in Whitchurch for this purpose within living memory.

A whooping-cough cure at Brailes was of more pleasant character. A turnip was sliced into three slices; these were placed one above the other in a pile with a layer of coarse sugar between each. The syrup draining from the stack of slices was given to the patient, and was probably soothing. Stratford infants were held nine mornings in succession over an odorous miskin. Possibly the strangest cure is the belief that anything recommended by a man riding a skew-bald horse would be a sure remedy. One gentleman, who possessed such an animal, declared that he was constantly begged to suggest something, and that he always said " Buttered ale."

Jaunders (Yellow Jaundice) was usually treated by some village quack who declared that he possessed an unfailing remedy; one of these consisted of the patient's urine flavoured with sugar, to which a little saffron had been added.

Shingles and Ringworm were anointed with dowment, the black grease from a church bell, but only that taken from the bearings of the great bell was efficacious. At Whitchurch a certain blacksmith named Bayley used, as a cure for shingles, grains of wheat roasted over his hearth in a shovel until the " oil " exuded; this oil was used to anoint the sufferer.

Sneezing may be lucky or unlucky as the case may be : if the sneeze is given to the right, it falls in the former category; if to the left, contrariwise. In our county, as elsewhere, it is customary to say to a person sneezing, " God bless you." This phrase was used in most remote times, and many tales are told to account for its origin, but none of them appear in any way adequate. In Warwickshire it would seem that the number of sneezes was more important than the position—

> One for wishing,
> Two for kissing,
> Three for a shocking bad cold.

Or in a longer and more modern form—

> One is a wish,
> Two is a kiss,
> Three is a disappointment.
> Four is a letter,
> Five something better,
> Six is a journey you'll go.　　(F. G. S.)

Again, there is the following rhyme that deals with sneezing—

> Sneeze on Monday, sneeze for a letter,
> Sneeze on Tuesday, something better;
> Sneeze on Wednesday, make a gift,
> Sneeze on Thursday, have a gift;
> Sneeze on Friday, sneeze for sorrow,
> Sneeze on Saturday, see your sweetheart to-morrow.
> If you sneeze on Sunday you will be a wicked person all
> 　　the rest of the week.

And the following, supplied by J. A. Langford—

> Sneeze on Monday, sneeze for danger,
> Sneeze on Tuesday, kiss a stranger;
> Sneeze on Wednesday, have a letter,
> Sneeze on Thursday, something better;
> Sneeze on Friday, sneeze for sorrow,
> Sneeze on Saturday, see your lover to-morrow.

For ordinary colds a few bulbs of the Crow-onion (*Allium viniale*) were taken, dried and powdered and enclosed in pieces of flannel to form a sock, which was placed in the patient's shoe.

Infectious diseases were terribly destructive of infant lives in the olden days, when disinfectants were largely unknown and consisted of burning aromatic herbs in a plague-pan; such pans, similar to the warming-pans, had perforated lids, and are far from uncommon. One in possession of Mr. Fox of Stratford has inscribed upon it: "Lord, have mercy on us."

In Stratford-on-Avon in 1915 an onion was suspended in a cottage under the impression that it would turn black if any member of the household were infected. In the autumn of this same year a few cases of scarlet fever occurred in Whitchurch, and one young mother told the writer she had pared an onion and buried the peelings where they could not be disturbed, and that this charm would carry the fever from the house.

The games of childhood, and such attempts at education as the times allowed of, are relegated to a later chapter, and the present must end with certain cures performed when puberty was reached and the dangers of more infantile complaints had passed by.

The most interesting of all these are the various charms for removing warts from the hand. These disfigurements are supposed to arise from washing in water in which eggs had been boiled. Fortunately in almost every place some person lived who could charm them away.

The objects used were various, but secrecy and a muttered incantation were an essential part of the programme. Some charmers affixed a piece of raw meat and secured it so that it could be carried home in contact with the wart, while the " wise man " worked the secret charm. On reaching home the meat must be buried, and its resting place kept a strict secret ; the wart would then disappear as the meat decayed. In another case the " wise man " touched the wart with his fore-finger and said something indistinctly, so that the potent words were inaudible to the patient. In this case some offering was essential, but it must not be money ; a marble, a button or any other of the miscellaneous trifles school-boys carry was gravely accepted, but the most efficacious was some object such as an old nail, or fragment of iron, found in the road whilst walking to the charmer's cottage. No expression of thanks must be offered or the effort would be in vain.

At Whimpstone in the parish of Whitchurch the great wart-charmer of fifty years ago was one John Day. His method was very simple. He looked at the patient's hand, did " something " with a knife to each wart and made a nick in a piece of stick taken from his wood pile, mumbling some words which were indistinct. The warts invariably disappeared. Unfortunately the writer's informant did not know what the stick was, or whether or not a cross was cut on the wart. Cures were attempted at home : for instance, warts were rubbed with black snails (*Limax maximus*), or the snail was impaled alive on a blackthorn spike, or pierced with a thorn and fastened in the earth. In either case, as the slug shrivelled the wart was supposed to decay. In another case the wart was rubbed for nine successive days with the inside surface of a broad-bean pod. The use of nine occurred also in one of the "black snail" versions : the patient was directed to rub the wart nine times each way with the slug. Another cure quoted in *E. D. D.* consisted in sticking a pin into an ash tree, then into the wart and again into the tree ; there it was left as a monument to the wart. An oil distilled from the ash is said to have been excellent for pimples. The most general vegetable cure was that of squeezing the white milk of the Sun Spurge on the wart. This cure is very widespread.

A styna on the eyelid was stroked with some gold object, usually a wedding-ring. This was done nine times, and the custom is widespread. According to another authority, the styna must be crossed with gold nine times, or, if gold be not procurable, the fur of a cat's tail must be rubbed backwards across it nine times in succession. This last operation is a Stratford custom.

CHAPTER VI.

Woman's Indoor Work : Baking.

One of the most picturesque adjuncts to the old-world cottage is the stone semi-circular oven, which usually stands out conspicuously at right angles to the line of walling, sometimes (though rarely) in the centre, but more generally at the gable end adjoining the hearth.

It has been suggested that its form may have some religious origin, but if so, it has been retained from practical necessity, and its advantage is the uniform diffusion of heat.

Opposite the door of the oven a large white or light-coloured stone was built into the wall ; this served the purpose of a rude thermometer, changing colour with the degree of heat as it became free from the deposit of carbon, which gradually burned away as the heating process proceeded, leaving the stone glowing at a white-heat, a marked object against its blacker neighbours. The mouth or door of the oven was closed by a shutter called the "Stopless," or in the north of the county "the Ditless." It was a massive piece of oak with two handles shaped to fit the entrance. When the oven had been heated and cleansed, and the bread inserted, the door or shutter was placed in the opening and the crevices round the stopless were stuffed up with wet rags ; when these were not available clay was used, or, in need, cow-dung.

The oven was heated by burning a faggot of thin cord wood, which was burnt on the floor of the oven. It was lighted in the centre and later pushed to one side ; this was done in order to prevent the fire from choking and thus hindering the heat from becoming equally diffused. The wood ashes were carefully preserved in order to make the lye for washing.

In the farms the supply of wood ash was insufficient, and wood ashes were brought round regularly by lye sellers. After the ashes were raked out into the receptacle made for them below the oven, and the floor very carefully wiped with a damp " daffle," or, as it was called in South Warwickshire, a " mawkein," or sometimes a " scovien " (this was a mop-like instrument made of scraps of cloth attached to a long handle by a swivel), any carelessness in this performance could be detected by the presence of small fragments of charcoal at the bottom of the loaves.

The dough for the weekly baking was mixed in a vessel known as a " dough kiver," which formed part of the furniture of every cottage. This consisted of an angular trough supported on a stand, and was sometimes of an ornamental character. It is not an uncommon object still, although the professional baker has largely taken the place of the domestic one.

The necessary quantity of flour was placed in the dough kiver and a small depression made in it, surrounded with a bank of flour. The barm was mixed to a batter with moderately hot water, but a red-hot poker or red-hot cinder was previously placed in it to remove the bitterness. It was then poured into the hole and mixed so that the flour fell in until the barm became properly thickened ; some dry flour was then placed at the top and the sign of the cross made in it to keep the evil influence of the witches aloof. The lid of the dough kiver was then shut down, and in the winter season a " bag " laid on the top to keep the dough warm. When the barm had done its work and the dough had risen, it was roughly kneaded by hand to prevent the formation of " coffins " (air spaces) in the bread, or the presence of small knobs of unkneaded dough called " lazy-backs " or " slut-farthings."

The dough was then made up into batch cakes, or loaves. The former consisted of any small portion of dough not sufficiently large to make a loaf, and where it was possible a little lard and sugar were added, when it became more like a cake ; these were also known as cobs, and in order to give them a thinner crust the dough was baked wrapped in cabbage leaves.

D

When baking at home ceased to be general, cakes were sent to the bake-house. Those of the different owners were distinguished by "docking." The docker was a piece of wood set with pointed wire of various designs, such as initials, or, where dockers were not at hand, by crosses incised with a knife.

Considerable care was needed in placing the loaves in the oven to economise space. This was done by means of the peel, a circular wooden (or iron) plate affixed at the end of a long shaft. The loaves were placed first on the floor, but not so that they touched one another and so caused "puffcrumbs" to form ; puffcrumbs were portions of loaf with no crust.

Then came the batch cakes, and sometimes "lard cakes" or "fleed cakes," folded after being thinly covered with lard. These were placed in front of the bread and near the mouth of the oven, and were of course the first to be removed. This required a second fitting of the stopless.

The batch cakes explain the proverb, "to go in with the bread, but to come out with the cakes." They were the precursors of the modern tea-cake, and were buttered and served hot. In families which made white bread only, it was usual to exchange a loaf with a neighbour making a brown or farmer's bread from whole wheat or seconds flour.

The bread when baked was kept in the "bread-pan," a large earthenware vessel covered with a moveable wooden lid, and placed in a cool, dry cellar, the quantity baked being sufficient to last until the next baking day. If by any chance this failed, "boughten bread" was obtained from the professional, but baker's bread was looked upon with contempt as something inferior, and the baking process at home was one the careful housewife was unwilling to delegate, and in any case gave constant oversight to every process, especially the work of the daffle and peel.

If by any chance through bad weather or other circumstances the big batch showed signs of going "ropey," or mouldy, the frugal woman of the farm would resolve on a "boiled bread" dinner, a resolution not received with enthusiasm by the younger members of the family. The bread was eaten with butter and salt. My authority adds : "Like Nebuchadnezzar's grass it might be wholesome, but it was not good."

There were certain cakes called wigs, made in various shapes, round and oblong as well as triangular, which were locally popular. A noted wig maker lived at Alcester who had a special reputation for the excellence of his wigs. In the ancient accounts in the P.R.O. of the College of St. Mary of Warwick they are mentioned as the chief food provided for a feast of the Dean and Canons held on Ascension Day. They are there termed wygge-brede.

The breakfast-hour on Sundays was later than other days, on which there was no fixed hour.

However, the hours in agricultural districts vary, not only in summer and winter, but also as between field work and barn or paid work, and on different farms. On one large farm in this district work begins at 6.30 in summer and at 7.0 in winter, breakfast being taken before leaving home ; at 10.0 is a break for half-an-hour for luncheon ; dinner at 1.0, tea at 5.0. Work ceases at 5.30.

In winter, dinner-hour was at 3.0 when working in fields, and no more work out of doors was done, but only in the barn or stable till 5.0.

Hogs' puddings were made from chitlings stuffed with cutlings. There was a mill at Atherstone-on-Stour, on the river-side, which is still called the Cutling Mill, which is a kind of coarse oatmeal used for pigs' food. It was formerly sold at a stall in Stratford Market and carried round the villages in a kind of double sack, one part holding cutlings, the other finer oatmeal. When the mill was disused for that purpose it was fitted up as a school. To return to hogs' puddings. The cutlings were boiled in milk and mixed with fat and a little pennyroyal. The boiling took a long time, and it was not until after this was finished that the stuffing took place. The puddings were apt to burst, but to prevent this mishap one of the parson's old wigs was suspended in the chimney; the less superstitious folk pricked them with a darning-needle.

WOMAN'S INDOOR WORK : BREWING.

In England at an early date beer was not brewed with hops, but with malt only. Hops were introduced from Flanders into the south of England about 1520. The strength of the beer brewed was settled, together with the rules relating to bread, by the Statute of 1266 (51 Hen. III., Stat. 1), by which a brewer neglecting the order was made liable to a fine. Offences specified were threefold : selling bad beer, too small beer, or selling in either unstamped measures or at a price contrary to that fixed by the assize. On every manor on which its lord had the right of assize, whoever brewed for sale was required to send for the manorial officers called aletasters, who named the price at which it could be sold. This was settled on a sliding scale, according to the price of the barley, and thus, when barley was sold at two shillings the quarter, beer was sold at a penny a gallon.

At the dawn of the fifteenth century (1405) various classes of ale were supplied in Stratford for the feast of the Holy Cross Guild. There was "gude beere 1½d., peneyale 1d., small ale ½d. a gallon," but in folk-lore there are many more names, and some of these are set out in folk rhymes which are fast disappearing. An Ilmington rhyme gives them as—

> Black strap,
> Ruffle-me-cap,
> Fine and clear,
> Table beer.

At Pillerton from a quarter of malt there was brewed—

> Twenty gallons of strong ale,
> Twenty gallons of table beer,
> Twenty gallons of small beer,
> Twenty gallons of Tit-me-Tat,
> Twenty gallons worse than that.

At Whitchurch two bushels of malt were said to have produced—

> Forty gallons of clink-me-clear,
> Forty gallons of table beer ;
> Forty gallons of Rat-me-Tat,
> Forty gallons worse than that.

At Alderminster, which is a Worcestershire parish only a mile from Whitchurch, a woman named Keyte, who had a reputation of being rather near, brewed—

> Double ale, single ale, very good ale,
> Twine-in-the-belly,
> Twice as many,
> Tip tap, worse than that.
> Pin.

She once gave a man tip-tap to drink, but on his laughing she was much offended, and requested the cause of such levity. The reply was : " Oi was a'wondering as how you could brew two worse."

Beer is commonly brewed still in the small farms and cottages in the south of the county, and is much stronger than that of the local brewery. In the old days the brewing took place in March and October, the later being the better. The implements consist of the mash-tub, the wort-tub and coolers ; the latter are large shallow tubs for cooling the liquors as they are run off at different strengths. The mash-rule is a wooden implement shaped like a gridiron, having a long handle, and is used for stirring the malt in the mash-tub. The wort ladder consisted of two short poles of wood, with two cross-pieces arranged ladder-wise in the middle of them, and was used to lay across the wort-tub to support the wood sieve through which the liquor was passed from the boiling copper to the tub.

The lade-gawn was a round wooden pail, one chine (stave) of it being carried up above the level of the rim and formed into a handle. The spigot and fawcet was a large wooden tap screwed through a hole in the wort-tub into the batwell or tap wad, a wicker-work sieve shaped like the covering of an oil flask. The tun-dish, a large circular pail of wood with a projecting circular spout from the bottom at its centre, to pass through the bunghole of a cask ; through this the cooled liquor was poured, and required care, as any amount saved at the spigot could easily be wasted at the bunghole as the cask filled.

Besides the beer, tilly willy was produced and used as a beverage for the younger members of the family.

In the March brewing an infusion of ale hoof (*Nepeta glechona*), Herif (*Galium aparine*) and shoots of the common nettle were added, and if the season advanced sufficiently a few young leaves of the Black Currant were prepared and passed through the mash-tub after the beer had been run off. Unlike the pure malt tilly willy of the October brewing, the March equivalent became Herb beer and was regarded as a drink preventive of " Spring rash."

After the products of the brewing had fermented, and the casks placed in the cellar in the upright position in which they were to remain, and had "worked" and the " barm " from each cask had passed from the bunghole through a barm-spout (a tube of either wood or metal which conveyed it clear of the top of the barrel, from which it fell into a receiving vessel), the bungs of the casks were closed, thick paper pasted over them and covered with a layer of wet sand ; a small hole at the top of one of the chines of the casks was left open until the flow of barm had ceased, when it was firmly corked. Pieces of iron, stored for the purpose, were then laid on the top of the casks to prevent the beer being soured by thunder.

After the brewing neighbours came in with crusts of bread and dipped them in the new beer; in later days cups were used. The custom was called " taking the first shot."

This is suggestive of the custom of Sops and Ale spoken of by the authorities.

To prevent the beer going " hard " a piece of washing

soda was put into the liquor as it boiled. This required care, as the addition of the soda would force the liquor violently upwards, and sometimes over the furnace, unless it was pushed down by the mash rower.

Sometimes a red-hot piece of iron was placed in the ale for the same purpose, being quenched in the liquor.

Sometimes about a gallon of wheat was tied in a bag and placed in the mash-tub to help strengthen the beer.

At the present day the cottagers use about $1\frac{1}{2}$ bushels of malt for a brewing, and make from 30 to 36 gallons. At the smaller farms 6 bushels are used.

The sleu is kept good by pouring about half-an-inch of beer over it and standing in a cold place. It will keep good this way for a month or more, but if it does not do its work properly get some stinging-nettles and rinse it up with it in the tub. Wheat flour is also used for this purpose. Some people put sugar in it, and when this was done it would not rise a second time. This mixture of sugar is one of the reasons why German yeast obtained a hold.

Among other species of beer appreciated locally may be named Stingo, a heavy beer made from wheat, and Mum, a beer brewed from malted wheat, very popular in the seventeenth century and introduced from Brunswick. Captain Yarrenton proposed to establish a brewery at Stratford for this beer.

Beer was also brewed from mangols, dandelions, coltsfoot, carrots, parsnips, and cowslips. From plums came the terribly strong Plum Gherkum, from rhubarb Rhubarb Whappy. Probably all of these are made by the cottagers of to-day.

Woman's Indoor Work : Washing.

Another important part of woman's work on the farm concerned the wash-tub. The washerwomen came overnight, laid the bucking, had a sup of gin, and went to bed. They rose between 3 and 4 o'clock, and for twenty-four hours the house was at their mercy. Soap, it appears, was little used, except as an auxiliary, its place being taken by the lye obtained from wood ashes, and already alluded to. The lye tub was a large circular tub having a moveable ladder resting across it, in the centre of which was a rectangular box or trough with slanting sides, perforated with a series of holes at the bottom ; in this was placed a tray filled with wood ashes wrapped in a hurden cloth, the whole kept filled up with boiling water, which percolated through the ashes into the tub below, driven by its weight. The lye was prepared on Thursday, the water was heated and the clothes washed through for the first time ; on Friday the washing was repeated, on Saturday they were washed for the third time and boiled, and all put in solution into the buck tub, the coarser things at the bottom, in layers, the finest at the top ; more water was then boiled and poured over the contents of the tub and then left over till Monday, when they were rinsed through, swilled, and hung out to dry. The buck tub had a spigot and fossit (prior to this invention a pig's jaw was used) to enable the water to be drawn off, which process was called "driving," a pewter plate was placed over the fossit to prevent the clothes being drawn in by suction. This done, the washerwoman could have her lunch. The great buck wash took place in the farms every nine or ten weeks, but there was a fortnightly ordinary wash, less ceremonial in its character. At Stratford clothes were boiled with a piece of suet or fat added before the lye was used, and a little lye kept from one wash to another, except on Good Friday, before which all was thrown away. No woman could wash on Good Friday.

In the *Book of Husbandry* of 1534 the duties of the farmer's wife are thus given : " The wyues winnowe, make malte, washe and wrynge, and make hay, shere corne, and in time of neede helpe to fyll the muck wayne, dryve the plough, loode haye, corne, and suche other, ride to market to sel hither butter, chese, mylke, egges, chekyns, capons, hennes, pygges, gese, and all manner of corne."

The farmer's wife rode behind her husband to market on a pillion. The writer once met an old lady who told him that her mother was the last person in the district to do so, and that long after it was discarded she had played with it as a girl. The old lady said it was fixed to the saddle by an iron hook, that the seat was tilted up, well stuffed, and nearly 4 inches thick. There was a handle behind which served as a back to the seat. The rider held on by placing her arms round her husband's waist. She remembered hearing that a certain farmer of Chacomb and his wife rode home from market one night in a somewhat fuddled condition. On their arrival the good man called lustily to his son, " Bob, come and help your mother down." Bob said, " Well, where is she ? " " Behind, you fool," replied his parent. " Some way behind, I think," answered Bob, " for she aint here." A lantern duly procured, search was made. The old lady had fallen into a ditch and " stanked up " the water, which had just begun to trickle over her. " Not a drop more to-night, thank you maister," she murmured as the rescuers arrived.

CHAPTER VII.

Death and Funeral Customs.

The mystery of death was usually to some extent prepared for in the village mind by various portents and warnings, sometimes extremely trivial in character, at other times merely natural phenomena, noticed and remembered by their coincidence with the decease of a member of the family.

Thirteen is, as everyone knows, an unlucky number; this is said to be due to the fact that Our Lord and his Apostles numbered thirteen at the Last Supper, but in reality much older. If it so chance that this unlucky number sit down to dinner together, the last to leave the table will die within twelve months, therefore an attempt was instituted to rise at the same instant; if this failed to satisfy nervous guests, the host would call attention to the number present, and retain his seat until the others had risen.

Such trivial things as a picture falling, or the flitch of bacon dropping from its hook in the chimney ingle, foretold an early death to some member of the family. So did the accidental ringing of a bell for no assignable reason, and the tapping of the Death-tick, a small beetle well known as *Anobium domesticum*, all of which have perfectly natural causes. At Whitchurch it is said that if a corpse lie in the parish over the Sunday another death will follow within the week. Langford says within a month. It is reported more definitely from Stratford-on-Avon. If at a funeral there chances to be present a Belgian horse, a variety of black colour, with flowing mane and tail, as most self-respecting undertakers' horses should have, and the animal turns his head and neighs at your door, there will be a funeral in the house within a year. (F. G. S.) Restlessness on the part of a horse, and his refusal to start with the hearse, is supposed to be in a similar way prophetical.

To the newly married funerals were most unlucky. Should the happy pair travel with a corpse with or without their knowledge, the death of one of them would be sure to result in a short time. *Certes*, the garb of woe and the presence of the dead are not fit companions for newly-wedded bliss, but short of infection it is hard to see the danger, nor can the idea be very old; one imagines funerals were hardly ever brought far in the old days, unless they chanced to be the embalmed bodies of kings and queens and other great folk.

The door of the house from which the deceased has been carried must not be closed until the return of the mourners, or another death will shortly follow, since you deserve such judgment for so soon forgetting those who have gone. It is always considered to bring bad luck to wear black to any extent before the actual funeral. Another unreasonable portent is thus expressed by Langford :—

> If in your house a man shoulders a spade,
> For you or your kinsfolk a grave is half made.

This rhyme seems to be doubtful in authority, especially as the point of the token lies in the spade being carried through the house from back to front, or *vice versa*. This was, of course, impossible where there was one door, and most old cottages had no more. Probably in most of these tokens and portents rarity of occurrence made the fact remarkable.

Birds flying against a window were deemed to be portents, and a rather interesting superstition is reported from Stratford. It is said, "Death is always about a house visited by a robin." Instances are known of the eggs and nest being destroyed for this reason, as the robin and wren were highly honoured and privileged, excepting only when they were systematically and ceremonially hunted and maltreated. (See Fraser's *Golden Bough.*) The opinion seems a strange one.

The generally diffused superstition of a winding-sheet on a candle, or a coffin thrown out of the fire, or a coffin in a loaf of bread all occur in the county, but call for no especial remark. Of a similar nature is the fear lest some backward fruit bud should extend itself into blossom out of season, though the occurrence is very common and a perfectly natural one.

If the hands of a dead person remain damp and clammy to the touch, it is a token that a death will quickly follow in the family. Moreover, if flowers are brought into a house, such as snowdrops, which droop their heads, it is a sign of death and bad luck. The writer in this way quite unconsciously caused the death of one of his flock ; Gastritis in an acute form was the real cause.

In South Warwickshire it is generally believed that the feathers of any game birds or pigeons, in the feather beds, bolsters, or pillows will cause the dying man prolonged and needless suffering. Quite recently at Whitchurch a man accused his wife of intentionally hindering his death in this way, though she assured the writer this was not the case. Why these feathers should be credited with this particular ill-will to the suffering man one has yet to learn, but the feather-bed is frequently removed from under the sufferer to ensure that no such ill-chance may happen.

Recently a Stratford lady of considerable mental attainment assured the writer that, before her husband died, for some weeks the newly-washed table linen showed a "diamond" in the centre, and however carefully the cloth was folded it could not be avoided. The trouble ceased with his death.

At Whimpstone the writer once bought a "grandfather" clock which had the reputation of striking wrongly ; thirteen was the number specified when any member of the family died. Strangely enough, at the death of Queen Victoria the clutch failed to act, and the clock certainly struck twenty-four, but this is the only clock superstition he has so far met with.

In some Warwickshire villages the better inhabitants kept specially fine linen sheets to cover over the dead, and these sheets often had an insertion of lace running up the middle and across the upper part, so that when folded down the two crossed one another and made in a way the Sign of the Cross. Such a sheet, seen by the writer at Whichford, was more than a century old. In any case, the sheet used for such a purpose had almost a reputation of sanctity. It was very considerably honoured for the length of service it had done. A sheet of like nature at Whatcote was only used for single women whose chastity was above suspicion.

It should not be forgotten that the general use of coffins is of comparatively modern date. The wealthy ecclesiastics of the Middle Ages and the great barons were buried in stone coffins, hewn out of solid masses of stone and having lids ornamented with the Holy sign, and sometimes in addition symbols of their rank. This was copied by wealthy merchants, and at length even the very poor were carried to rest in coffins of wood. At first there was a parish coffin with a detachable bottom, that portion only being left behind in the grave. Under all these circumstances it was only decent and proper that the deceased should be covered with a pall. It is a great pity that this ancient practice has so nearly ceased. It is not necessary that the pall be hideous or grotesque, as most old-fashioned funeral customs were, and often, moreover, wickedly extravagant to boot. For instance, the bill of a village mechanic as late as 1878 contained the following items :—

> 13 silk and 4 crape hat bands at 6s. 6d. or 7s. 6d. each ; 20 pairs of gloves for men, including the clergyman, clerk, sexton and two drivers, a total of £2 8s., and seven pairs of gloves for women at £1 1s.

One can but shudder at the cost of a man's interment in those days, and the very thought of the display is appalling.

There was a custom that sprang up in the eighteenth

century of stationing a lugubrious individual in black,
called a mute, on the doorstep of a house containing a
dead man. This person held in one hand a kind of glori-
fied mop, with long black streamers to match the hatband,
which drooped from his high hat nearly to his feet. The
more miserable he looked the better his chances of employment. Surely our immediate forefathers had strange
tastes and were extraordinarily morbid. The skulls,
cross-bones and symbols of decay bear witness to this
on the gravestones. Of christian hope there was little
or none.

We have already seen that a funeral crossing the path
is a sign of death to the bride or bridegroom, but it is
generally considered unlucky. One would suppose such
occurrences along the road to the cemetery of a large
town would render life in its neighbourhood exceedingly
precarious, but it can be avoided by turning one's back on
the funeral cortège. (F. G. S.)

It has been stated that if the grave is left open over
the Sunday another death will follow; but surely such an
event could seldom or never have happened, especially in
those days when body-snatching was common.

The earliest burial customs of which we have any
detailed knowledge in these islands are those of the
people who buried their important folk under a long
barrow. These mounds were of two kinds: in the one,
chambers were constructed of large stones, and were
possibly copies, artificially constructed, of the earlier
caves in which interments were first made. In their
earliest form they were cells constructed of three or more
stones, with a cap stone above them, and the whole was
covered with earth, which in course of ages has often
gone and the cromlech alone is left; round this a wide
range of folk-lore tradition has gathered, but as none
of these tumuli exist in our county they need not be
discussed here.

In a later form a series of chambers or cells were
constructed with a view to continuous use. The bodies
of the dead were placed in these receptacles unburnt, as a

rule, though all along cremation was also practised. The early people seemed to have lived in terror of the return of the ghost of the dead man to take possession once more of his wives, goods and chattels. For this reason a ghost hedge was placed round the edge of the mound, and the body of the deceased was either disjointed or burnt to ensure the destruction of his form and prevent his ghost from its malignant work.

The long barrow was in time superseded by the round barrow, and the interments therein are usually cremated and the ashes placed in an urn buried below the mound ; objects were buried with the deceased for his use in the after world, and such objects are still occasionally interred, but not, of course, with any but a sentimental idea. On Brailes hill the barrow contained amber beads, and a few other instances are noted in the *Victoria County History of Warwickshire*. This county has alas preserved few of its early monuments—it is too well cultivated.

This short note has been written because we still use the grave mound in our churchyards and cemeteries, and the interments, as in the case of the Long Barrow, are orientated, that is, the deceased is placed facing the rising sun, in all probability a pre-Christian idea.

It must not be forgotten that the north side of the churchyard was rarely if ever used in villages, except for the burials of suicides and the unbaptized. It lay in the shade, away from the sun. In almost every old church-yard the more ancient stones will be found on the south. Headstones were not at all common at an early date ; the oldest inscribed stone of this class in the county known to the writer is one at Brailes dated 1600, but body stones of an earlier date may be found at Binton, where they cover the length of the grave and bear the form of the floreated cross, the chief and commonest decoration of early coffin lids. In South Warwickshire there are large numbers of boldly carved headstones hailing from Edgehill district, and much in request during the latter half of the seventeenth and the first quarter of the eighteenth century. They consist of sunk or raised panels, either rectangular, circular or oval and convex, surrounded by conventional foliage, curtains, cherubim, and emblems of mortality. More rarely they are pierced, so that the sides of the stone are carved with the twisted columns peculiar to the style of late Renaissance, or they have portrait medallions of the deceased. Sometimes they are even more ambitious, and attempt full lengths in the round. As a whole they are boldly cut and the designs are good. They were succeeded by tombstones of far lighter design, with swags of flowers and urns in low relief in Chippendale and Adams style, and these in turn by stones on which are incised patterns that form an intricate ornament, and must have required considerable technical skill. These gave way to the Victorian cross-type, which is still in general use. Many of these early stones have home-made epitaphs upon them, but very few are really quaint. They are an exhibition of lamentably unorthodox theology, and often enough glaringly egotistical advertisements of the deceased's good works.

There is a popular notion that any path taken by a funeral party bearing the corpse with them becomes a public right-of-way, and in this connection many of the paths leading from outlying hamlets to the mother church were called "church-ways," "corpse-ways," or burial-paths. Such paths are plentiful at Stratford; a path from Wilmecot leading from that hamlet, the chapel of which was the property of the Holy Cross Guild, has become a right-of-way through this cause.

Frequently in law-suits respecting right-of-way the fact that a corpse has been carried along the route without any objection has been alleged. Shottery Road is still called "Berrin Road" by the old people of Stratford; while church roads ran from Fulready, Thornhill and Upper Ettington to the old church by the hall, long since disused, in a perfectly straight line, and a similar path still exists at Whitchurch from the small outlying hamlet of Bruton.

The strangest legend of the kind hails from Brailes,

where it is said a right-of-way exists over Brailes hill, because the dead of Brailes were taken to Bredon to be buried by that path.

This looks like the survival of the reputation of some ancient sacred way, for it is quite certain that in historical times no person from Brailes would have been carried to Bredon, to be buried, by such an impossible path.

CHAPTER VIII.

The Husband and Wife.

When the woman of the farm and cottage was not busy healing her children by strange charms and old-world cures which savour almost invariably of the medicine-man of some primitive tribe, she was as busy as any slave could have been to further the interests of her lord and master.

Let the words of old Fitzherbert tell in their own concise way the sum of her daily life, altered, it is true, in some details, but which is not wholly inadequate as the description of a cottager's home life of to-day. It begins :—

Lyfte up thy hands and blesse thee, and make a sygne of the Holy Crosse—and remember thy Maker, thou shalt spede muche the better—then first swepe thy house, dresse up thy dyshe borde, and sett all thynges in good order within thy house—mike thy kye, secte thy calves, spy up thy milke, take up thy chyldren and arraye them and provyde thy husbandes brekephaste, dynner, souper, and for thy chyldren and servantes, and take thy parte with theyen and to ordeyne, come and walke to thy mill, and to bake and brue, withall where nede is, and meete it to the myll, and fro the mylle, and se that thou have thy measure agayne, besyde the tolle—thou must make butter, and chese, when thou maist, serve thy swine, both mornynge and evenynge, and gyve thy poleyn meate in the mornynge and when tyme of the yeare commeth thou must take hede how thy hennes, duckes and geese do ley, and gather up theyre eggs and when they waxe broodye, to sette them there as noo beastes swyne nor other varmyn harte them.

Much of this has drifted away from the farm to the cottage, but in both brewing is still done, and in some the nearly lost art of baking is reviving. The house-cleaning operations are deferred till the noon or even later, for the children must be sent off to school, and their food, if they have far to go, must be packed and taken, and the husband's food also; but an older woman will still rise at four or five to get her husband some warm drink such as tea or chocolate before he starts to his toil.

Few possess calves, and milking by women is little more than a tradition, but in other respects, such as serving the swine and feeding the poultry, there is little change. The women, moreover, were expected to assist in the field and help to reap and gather in the crops, and even if need be to load the muck wain, but of this more anon. Certes the good woman had little time for either newspapers or novels had such things been in her way in the days of Fitzherbert, which happily they were not.

What recreation she had was either found at church or the market, or else in some of the many village festivals, which have so entirely disappeared.

Probably the farmer's wife of the old days was on the whole a proud and happy woman, too busy to be discontented, and desiring only to be a good housewife and to be held in repute for her good cheer and the number of her progeny.

A local celebrity who had a mind set on rhyme (a by no means rare event in the old days) was rather addicted to matrimony. His three ventures were successively mean, good, and ill-tempered. He is said to have expressed himself thus :—

> God bless pritchitee patch,
> Likewise Save-all,
> And the devil take Tear-all.

If by rare ill-luck the matrimonial compact was an unhappy one, the neighbours knew well how to deal with the offender. The voice of public opinion made itself heard in the blunt, rude and unpleasant manner laid down by immemorial custom, and such instances are still to be found.

A man might be, and perhaps often was, a cruel husband, thrashing his wife with scant mercy. In such a case the neighbours strewed his doorstep with chaff during the night, as a public advertisement to the fact that he

E 2

had been thrashing his corn overnight. This custom has been practised within recent years in many places.

Drunkenness was looked upon with much tolerance, and even at times with praise and commendation, and the amount consumed by the village toper was often enormous. As an extreme instance the writer was reliably told that Samuel G. of Wimpstone could drink as much as a gallon of beer at a time, and would quaff off a quart without taking breath. On one occasion he is said to have drank two gallons lying on his back by the roadside. It is not very astonishing to learn that he ended his days in the county asylum.

A certain local pig-killer told me with pride that he became very ill from drinking more ale than he could wisely take—not, he explained, "too much," but more than was good for him. He at length was compelled to visit a medical man, who told him to drink cyder and plenty of it. His reply was, "Well, I do drink eighteen quart a day; how much be I to drink?" One can imagine that a man in that state might beat his wife at times. In his case she did the beating.

Domestic infelicity leading to adultery was rare, for one thing during the Middle Ages the church was very strict in its condemnation of incontinency in any form, and the lord of the manor, being responsible for the heavy fines paid by the offender, was equally so; moreover, an illegitimate child was a loss to him manorially, as such could not be claimed as the child of a servile father. Marriage, as we have seen, was so extremely easy that incontinence was rare. It was far different during the post-Reformation period.

For the moment, however, we are dealing with adultery and its village cure. At an extremely early age a man could slay another who had robbed him of his honour, but this was softened down to emasculating him, and that in turn into a more vicarious method of burning the guilty pair in effigy. This custom has survived within living memory in many Warwickshire villages, an instance of which occurred some years since at Whatcote. On this occasion effigies of both parties were carried in procession by the villagers, accompanied by the music of beaten pots, pans, shovels, and anything that could be made to produce discordant noises. In the Whatcote instance a coarsely dramatic representation of the offence was made at stated intervals on the route, stones were hurled through the windows of the offender's house, and the effigies, which were exceedingly gross, were burnt before his windows. In the Whitchurch example only one effigy was so carried. This custom of Low-belling is recorded from Priors Marston, and is probably general not only in the county of Warwick, but outside its limits.

A less aggravated form, used not only for adultery but for any unpopular movement, is found in the rough music of the villages. The effigies are no longer present, merely the procession with its discordant noises and ribald shoutings. It has been used in the county for a wife-beater, a master who had harshly dismissed a servant, and even in a more impersonal manner to mark disapproval of a magisterial decision. In workshops and factories in towns, noisy tools and implements supplied the place of domestic pots and pans, and were used indiscriminately to express either approval or disapproval. In the days of apprenticeship the completion of indentures was sometimes heralded in this manner, and was the summons to the payment of the footing the ex-apprentice was expected to provide on attaining his freedom. (E. S.)

Fraser, in the *Golden Bough*, had traced in his own matchless language the steps backward, from the effigy to the living animal, until the original human sacrifice of the offender duly appears. There is small doubt that Loobelling or Low-belling is a late survival of the actual sacrifice of the human offender at the hands of the tribe.

In this connection it must not be forgotten that there is still an idea that a wife may be legally sold. Maitland cites a case in 1302, in which a woman had been quit-claimed to a man. In this case the conveyance was by charter, but in our villages wife-sales took place in the

open market. The price must be one, two, or three
half-crowns, and he must lead her prior to the sale
through three turnpike gates or through as many villages,
and must pay the toll. There does not appear to have
been any moral stigma attaching itself to the woman who
has been bought. The custom, despite the embroidery
of turnpike gates and tolls, would seem to have been of
great antiquity. It suggests that the wife is a slave to be
sold at will, as, in fact, children under age could be sold,
and is yet another link to extreme antiquity. (F. S. P.)

It was formerly part of the duty of churchwardens to
present to the Bishop cases, either proved or suspected,
of incontinence and adultery, and the offenders were cited
to appear before the Consistory Court, no small punishment in itself in days when travelling was anything but
easy. If found guilty they were excommunicated in
sonorous phrases and with due solemnity, and could only
receive absolution after public confession and penance.
The penitent, clad in a white sheet and holding a lighted
candle, declared his or her crime in the parish church
during divine service—a return to which happy state the
Commination service says "is greatly to be desired."
One rather pities would-be churchwardens if the reform
is really brought about.

If our typical rustic and his wife altogether escape
the perils of the matrimonial journey they will probably
jog along life's road together and make, as wise folks, the
best of it. Perhaps she will cure his drunken ways by
putting a live eel in his favourite beverage (F. S. P.),
and perhaps he may not be unduly severe with the rod,
or perhaps it may chance that she be mentally and
physically the stronger, and will bear the sway to the
end; but in any case in time old age will bring its
troubles, and the ills of cramp and rheumatism will affect
them. For these there are a number of rather curious
charms, which are worthy of a place in this work.

Cures for rheumatism usually took the form of carrying
some object in the pocket, and some of these simple things
can hardly by any stretch of imagination be credited with

efficacy. A piece of potato worn hard and glossy was carried by a Stratford man for twenty years as a charm against the screws. The gall of the wild rose, the exceedingly beautiful Fairy pincushion, is similarly carried; and at Whimpstone another gall insect which causes swellings on the common Field-Thistle is used. The thistle is known to all our older men as the "Cramp Thistle."

A well-known ancient cure is that of allowing bees to sting the affected parts. F. G. S. states that a bee-keeper of his acquaintance lost two hives in this way, through disturbing them to oblige his friends. There is perhaps some genuine efficacy in the cure, but it is one not likely to become popular.

Some of the cramp cures have a certain amount of merit, in other cases they are very similar to those used for rheumatism. Four different practices are in use at Whichford : to draw the fingers between the toes and to smell them ; to turn the sufferer's boots so that the soles are uppermost ; to carry a cork in the pocket, and, in like manner, to carry a "cramp bone" taken from a leg of mutton. This last is in widespread repute.

F. G. S. notes a cure for pins and needles which is of some interest. The sufferer is required to wet his finger and make the sign of the cross on the top of his boot. The action would no doubt help to restore lost circulation, but the ceremonial can hardly be modern.

There is nevertheless sound truth in an old Ilmington adage—

> If you'd live to be old
> Strip before you sweat
> And dress before you're cold.

This rhyme, which hails from an old native of Ilmington parish, of course alludes to the practice always followed by him of throwing off the outer garments for field work in summer time. Women stripped to the petticoat for field work up to the quite early part of the nineteenth century, but not later.

CHAPTER IX.

Dress.

On a general survey of the dress of the rustic population of England for the past thousand years, one learns
that the modern attempt made by the serving-wench of
to-day to copy her mistresses' latest gowns and hats is no
new thing. In the past, as now, the village belle aped
her betters, and the village beau, his employers; but at a
period when money was non-existent so far as the country
folk were concerned, and the means of spending practically nil, custom very largely ruled, and the clothes worn
on the working days were very much identical in form
for one generation after another. Indeed it was of
practical necessity that clothing should be of the simplest
character, since the wearer spent most of his life "hockling
over the clats" and tending sheep and cattle. The Saxon
theow wore no hat, his shoes were simple, his coat the
tanned hide of one of his charges; a leather belt girded
his coat and discounted its misfit; his stockings were
home-spun and home knitted, and worn cross-gartered.
The women folk wore long gowns reaching to the feet, a
practice which no amount of common-sense, until quite
lately, has entirely set aside ; their hair was entirely
concealed, whilst for several centuries it was reckoned
indelicate to allow the hair to be visible. This type of
costume held its own well into the thirteenth century,
when a short cloth tunic, short loose breeches and a cap
took its place. In the following century the fantastic
costume of the gentry descended to those beneath them ;
queer hoods with a pendant tail called a "liripipe" were
worn by all classes ; pointed shoes were a mark of the
period, but the good folk we treat of could hardly have
worn them with comfort, and the women even were
obliged to loop up the skirts of their long sweeping

kirtles and protect them with a "barme-cloth," or, as we should say nowadays, an apron.

They covered their hair with a wimple and peplum, of which the servant's cap may perhaps be a survival. The boots of the peasantry were made of untanned leather and called cockers. By the middle of the century hats replaced caps and ploughmen wore socks, though reapers, carters and others do not appear to have indulged in this luxury. The short tunic and loose knickers were probably in general use. In the reign of Richard II. the women of England began to show their hair, and it was never after this entirely concealed. The earlier custom is still preserved in Nunneries and Sisterhoods, and takes us back to those remote days when any such exposure was deemed immodest.

During the fourteenth century agricultural labourers might have been seen toiling in parti-coloured costumes, half of one colour and half of another, and the sleeves counter-changed ; but most of the extravagances of its latter days were passed by so far as the country folk were concerned. From the fifteenth century onwards boots of a simple form were worn, stockings, short breeches, and tunics well girded with a simple leather belt, while hats of various forms supplanted the older capuchon. At its close we learn that the well-to-do husbandmen wore breeches woven from sheep's wool, stockings of white kersey, high buckled shoes, a russet coat fastened with a white leather belt, a turned-down linen collar, and a cap with flaps. In the early days of Elizabeth, ruffs, both at the neck and wrists, were worn by the peasantry, and a white kerchief was pinned across the breast, while the hat was a stiff and serviceable one. Later on the women distended their skirts on frames and the men wore trunk hose. The doublet and hose held their own in slightly varying forms through the sixteenth and seventeenth centuries. It is only within living memory that colour has been abolished ; men still living can almost remember the farmer of their childhood wearing on Sundays a blue coat with brass buttons, a yellow waist-

coat, and high collar and cravat, while the memory of
the early-Victorian crinoline and coal-scuttle bonnet is
still more green.

In a few families old wedding garments are preserved,
illustrating the high waist and low necks of the early
days of the nineteenth century, but none of these things
really concern the folk-lorist.

The folk survivals in the matter of dress are not very
numerous, but such as they are they prove to be very
interesting. First in importance is the smock-frock of
the labourer, a garment reaching nearly to the knees, and
having a hole to put the head through. The yoke,
elaborately embroidered in wheel or other patterns, handed
down by local tradition ; it was attached to the main
portion of the garment by pleats, elaborately honey-
combed ; the cuffs of the sleeves were similarly treated.
These garments were worn within living memory. One
was always reserved specially for Sunday wear ; this was
rather more elaborately treated and of finer linen. The
garment was supposed to be derived from the twelfth-
century "Bliaut," which was made of coarse canvas or
fustian, and with no very definite shape, and it was worn
during inclement weather. The smock-frock for men
and the apron for women are undoubtedly of great
antiquity ; the apron was also called either a barme-cloth
or a napron.

The dress of working men as still recollected consisted
of knee breeches of cord-du-Roy below the knee, blue
stockings, knitted from homespun yarn, yellow leggings,
and thick boots. Their head-gear for Sundays was the
beaver hat ; when this went out of fashion a soft billy-
cock made of coarse frieze was worn instead, and to
the present day straw hats are not used ; a soft billy-
cock of the old type is general. Over the smock-frock
the wallet was hung, a long strip of linen passing over
both shoulders and hanging down in front ; at either
end were capacious pockets, in one of these the food was
carried and in the other "the drink."

As an accessory of dress mention must be made of

the staff, probably originally a simple stake or sapling, but at later date not infrequently ornamental. A stout staff of oak with curved handle served the village elders, a sapling of ash or hazel the younger men—on these were carved intricate patterns worked out in chip-carving, and at times the initial of the owner ; or fancifully contorted sticks, which had for some natural reason had a peculiar growth such as would strike the eye, were adapted for the new purpose, but probably at no time, even on holidays, were sticks habitually carried.

CHAPTER X.

FARM BUILDINGS.

The farm-yard of the middle of the nineteenth century had usually in its midst a heavily framed feeding crib of a square form. The round form, surmounted by a conical thatched roof supported on posts, as seen in Oxfordshire, is not, so far as the writer is aware, known in this county, but the square form was thatched at times, sometimes as a temporary measure, at others permanently. The rack below was kept supplied with hay and clover, though in modern practice most of the feeding is done in the fields, and "cake" and roots form the principal fare. The yard feeding in a modern farm is done with stalls fitted with mangers along one side of the cow-house or stable, as the case may be.

In these portions of the county where building stone was not easily obtainable, the cow-sheds, ox-stalls, or byre were largely of wood, with wood supports in front, and thatched. In the stone districts the walls and supports were of stone. Some of the carters' hovels and ox-stalls at Tysoe and Oxhill still retain these remarkable specimens of masonry. The stone columns supporting the ridge poles are built of small squared blocks, and taper from the base upwards.

The chief feature, however, of the farm-yard was the barn. A wonderfully fine range of stone-built barns is still in use at Whatcote, but there is no important tithe barn such as Worcestershire affords at Bredon and Littleton. The medieval timber barn had low side walls, often of the normal height of the old English cottage, viz., six feet, and from this the vast roof rose perhaps sixty feet or more, one great expanse of thatch, supported by timber columns and cross-beams in a rude manner not unlike a church. The stone-built barns were more pretentious, and were roofed in the stone districts with stone slates. There are, however, two other classes of old barn. The one consists of a timber frame to which rough axe-hewn boards have been attached ; the other type had the spaces filled in with wattle and daub, or in later periods with brick. Of these two, the former is said to be best to store corn in, as it allows the air to penetrate more freely than in any other description of barn. They are, however, so hostile to the modern idea of the trim farm that they will soon be few and far between. A good specimen at Wimpstone was blown down in the gale of January 1916. Barns were often kept for especial use : thus one hears of the Mow Barton for hay, the Barley Barn, etc., but the expression Barton, widely used for the buildings and even land of the farmstead, is by Warwickshire use confined to the enclosed farm-yard. A loft for storage of hay over the stabling is called a " tallet."

The granary is of necessity on an upper floor, and approached usually by an external stone staircase; the floors were formerly cemented with gypsum, which was extensively quarried for the purpose in the Alcester neighbourhood. Malting was often illicitly carried on in the house, and when the practice was usual some of the rooms in the upper story, or even in the space immediately within the roofing, were cemented, and wooden bins constructed. The malt and corn were raised and lowered in bags by pulleys of wood, an example of which may still be seen in the farm at Lower Milcote, built out of the ruins of Milcote House soon after the Civil War. Malting bins and flooring are still in evidence above the Roman Catholic chapel within the old Rectory House of Brailes, in old mansions at Ettington and Long Marston, and probably in many other places. This concealment was due to the strict laws conserving the grain supply made in the reign of Queen Elizabeth and later, on more than one occasion.

In the farm, as different to the cottage, a very important room was the dairy. It had to be cool and accessible and convenient. It must also contain provision for milk pails and for butter, and all must be kept clean, or the milk would turn sour. The dairy was the

portion of the homestead that the farmer and his wife
were in constant anxiety about, because it was easily
"witched." If the supply of milk failed, if any particular cow became unexpectedly barren, if the butter
would not come—in all these cases some unfortunate old
woman of the village was suspected, and often enough
cruelly treated, because she had laid a spell on the farmer.
Such tales are plentiful, and more than half believed in
even nowadays.

Cows were milked by women well within living
memory, and there are still some who know the art ; the
picturesque milkmaid is no longer seen. On Brailes
hill, and probably elsewhere, the cows were not led home
to be milked, but the milking pails were carried to them
and the milk brought home—a very severe labour. The
first milk from a cow after calving was considered a great
delicacy ; it was called " cherry curds," and used to
make a special pudding of the same name. The customary time allowed for new milk to stand, preparatory
to skimming, was from twelve to twenty-four hours; it
was then skimmed, that is, the cream was removed with
a brass perforated skimmer, a saucer-shaped utensil with
a slightly hollowed bowl. A quart of cream was
expected to make a pound of butter, but in practice it
failed. In the modern dairy it requires more. The old
idea prevalent well into the nineteenth century taught
that cows yielded more milk if they were milked by
women rather than men, since they were more amenable
to the softer and gentler handling. The essential instrument in milking was the see or sye bowl to strain the
milk. It was a circular bowl, shaped with a bottom of
fine gauze, set in a frame ; this was so constructed that
the milk percolated through the gauze and escaped into
a receiver, from which it made its way into the pan
by passing through the legs of the stand, which were
hollowed from about half their height.

The cream, after salting, was made into butter once
a week in a churn ; of this essential machine there were
several varieties. Throughout the medieval period, when

the cooper was in his glory, everything possible was made of wood—buckets, tubs and churns. The churn stood on the floor ; it was circular in form with slanting sides, and the cream was stirred by the movement of a churn pole, which ran perpendicularly through the lid of the churn and acted as a piston, with upward and downward movement.

The production of small quantities of butter up to a pound was managed either by enclosing the cream in a bottle and shaking it, or by the use of a box-churn. This was set upon a table when in use, and followed two forms : in one the beaters were arranged round the churn staff, which was moved vertically by hand ; in the other they were set on an axle, and revolved by turning a handle. The churn still in general use is the barrel churn. The beaters are set in a frame so as to be revolved horizontally. A variety called an " End over End Churn " had no beaters, but was set in a frame so that it could be revolved vertically.

As already hinted, the real danger to the successful issue of the labour of churning lay in the butter being "witched." There were two methods of dealing with such a predicament. If matters were serious, and the witch had herself passed into the vessel, a poker was heated red hot, and after two or three turns of the handle thrust into the opening. In less severe cases kinder measures were resorted to. A silver spoon or a piece of silver money was thrown in, witches happening to have an antipathy to silver ; this was usually effective.

As a rude rhyme the following was in use at Ettington :—

> Churn butter, churn,
> Come butter, come,
> The great bull of Banbury
> Shan't have none.

As the words were recited a poker was stamped upon the ground, keeping time to the metre.

Another dairy article was the milk-lead, a long rectangular vessel similar in form to a salting-lead, but

not so deep. It rested on the "thrawl" of the dairy
and was filled with milk, so that it might cool and set ;
when the cream had "risen" to the surface of the milk
it was skimmed off with a skimming dish and the milk
emptied out of the lead. This form is practically obsolete.
Another form was much smaller, and nearly square-
shaped. It was mounted on a wooden frame and the
milk drawn off from under the cream by an outlet and
tap at the bottom. This was the immediate precursor of
the modern separator.

At Tanworth, Wootton Wawen, and probably elsewhere it was customary for the larger farmers to give the
whole yield of milk from the dairy cows on Whitsun Eve
to the cottagers living near. At Tanworth the custom
was in use until 1870 or so, when the milk from fourteen
cows was in this way distributed. It began to be disused
when the custom was claimed as inviolable, and demands
were made that it was difficult or impossible to comply
with. Ebrington, a Gloucestershire village adjoining
Ilmington, had a curious charity left by a seventeenth-
century philanthropist, by which two farms were charged
with the duty of furnishing a certain number of milch
cows each summer, which were apportioned by the churchwardens to certain cottage families. The duty of milking
rested with the recipients. Hence, in the old days of
milkmaids Ebrington girls were in request as expert
milkers.

Cheese made at South Warwickshire farms was collected and sent in loads to various large cheese fairs.
The principal mart for South Warwickshire was the great
fair at Chipping Sodbury in Wiltshire. Each waggon-
load of cheese had a guardian spirit or mascot, as we
should now term it, in the form of a cheese made to
resemble a hare in its form, coloured to represent nature ;
the colours were obtained from marigolds, sage, and the
natural colour of the cheese. Such a hare surmounted
every load. (F. S. P.)

The old-fashioned cheese press was an upright instrument of strong beams, and the weight consisted of a

rectangular block of stone, adjusted so that it could be raised or lowered. Very few of these presses exist to-day, but the massive stones are common enough objects, since they are practically indestructible. A special form of cheese was also made with thin layers of chopped sage at intervals ; this was one of the delicacies used at shearing feasts, and is very savoury and delicious, though fast dying out.

Cheeses were stored within the homestead in a special room called the cheese room, the floor of which was cemented with gypsum ; it was usually on an upper story, dry and well ventilated.

CHAPTER XI.

The Farm-house and Cottage.

Our work would be very incomplete if no mention was made of the buildings in which the farmer and his servants lived. Neither is it possible to neglect the more humble cottage.

In the Middle Ages there was probably no very great line of demarcation between them, and the origin of the one is the origin in like manner of the other. In these islands, after men had given up their resort to caves, and indeed during the cave-dweller period, a simple circular excavation in the ground, carefully roofed-in, supplied the home. These pit-dwellings deserve a moment's attention.

A space was hollowed out in the ground, sometimes as large as thirty feet in diameter, but usually very much smaller ; the soil was removed to a depth of six or seven feet and the bottom was made reasonably dry by a thick layer of sand ; the sloping sides were pitched with large stones, and the whole roofed-in with boughs of trees turfed over and thatched in such manner that the roof was pyramidal in form. Entrance was obtained by an inclined pathway leading downwards to the floor level, and upon this floor two large stones were placed to serve as a support for the earthen cooking jar.

The smoke found its way out as best it could. The simple instruments of housewifery consisted of pounding-stones for bruising the corn, and a flat stone to bruise it upon. Very similar stones heated to a red heat were dropped into the cooking vessel to heat the water. Such knives as were in use were of chipped flint, as were the awls and needles by which skins of wild animals were adapted to the purpose of clothing ; articles of wood and horn were doubtless also used.

The first improvement upon these very primitive dwellings obviated the labour of hollowing out the earth, and avoided the dampness and obscurity of an underground dwelling. A circle of poles fastened together at the top was erected ; the omission of a few poles gave a simple doorway, and the whole was covered with heather, bracken or some similar substance turfed over. Here and there in our island, wherever charcoal burners work, this form of rude dwelling can still be seen. It must be noted that the turf is placed with the grassy side inwards, otherwise the loose earth would be for ever falling on the inmates and their food.

Excavations upon the site of a celtic lake-dwelling settlement at Glastonbury take the inquirer a long way forward. Here, within a palisaded enclosure, stood seventy or more huts, the homes of a comparatively civilized race, experts in the use of metal and wood work. The huts were erected on platforms supported upon piles, and were for the most part circular in form and constructed with stout poles in a form of wickerwork, and in what we moderns should term wattle and daub. At each entrance was a flat stone, and other similar slabs formed a hearth. The most interesting point is that the walls were upright, giving at once more space and air. The roof was probably thatched and conical in form. All the huts were moreover not circular, a few were rectangular and had walls six feet in height, the traditional height of the side walls of an old English cottage.

It was not a very far cry from these huts to the first beginnings of the old English cottage. These may be traced chiefly in Wales and the adjoining borderland. Here the shepherd population had winter and summer houses. The latter, mere booths, were constructed of two pairs of poles interlaced at the top, and a fifth pole laid horizontally from fork to fork, the whole being thatched in, the thatch being affixed to pairs of smaller poles set at suitable distances between the end pairs. In the more permanent dwellings the poles became trees called crucks or crocks, and such a dwelling of two pairs of crocks, ridge pole and rafters, formed a house of one bay, which could obviously be extended to any length by the addition of more crocks and rafters.

It must be noted that men did not build their dwellings at haphazard to suit their own particular use and convenience as we moderns do. They had Aryan custom to contend with, and that custom enjoined that a bay must contain sufficient standing-room for the small team of four oxen ; it must be sixteen feet in length.

The construction of a single bay was simple enough. The two pairs of crocks or gavel forks, from which our word "gable" is derived, were tied together by a ridge pole and strengthened by wind braces and beams. It was then thatched in from the ridge poles to the grounds. There were no walls and no windows, but an opening in lieu of a door at one end. The alteration from a slanting roof to the upright walls of a cottage was a very important one, and its evolution was not difficult. The tie-beams had at first stretched merely across the gavel forks, but they were now extended until a line dropped from their ends and touched the outer of the crocks. From these extended end-beams were laid the whole length of the bay, and were afterwards known as wall plates. Rafters were then laid from them to the ridge pole, and corresponding uprights set to meet them from the ground to the wall plate. Sometimes these were placed side by side in juxtaposition, sometimes a space was left ; if so, this space was filled up with a rough wickerwork of laths plastered over with mud. Later on the space grew larger and was filled in with wattle and daub, stud and mud, clan-stuff and daub, as the case might be. These fillings have often been replaced time and again, and may be seen commonly enough bricked up. The frame-work of a house is often far older than its walls.

Houses built with gavel forks, as here described, are very rarely preserved, but some of a form nearly approximating to it may be met with in outlying districts, such as the Tysoe district. In time the type of roofing formed from the beams and ring-posts did away with the more primitive crucks, and first came into use in the cottages built with mud walls, without a frame.

These had doorways in the side and not in the gable,

and the door had a screen within to keep off the wind; this was a very needful precaution when the door was merely a curtain of harden. In the more luxurious dwellings an upper room was constructed, and access to it was obtained by a ladder leading to a trap door.

The enlargement of a house was not confined to the addition of bays. There is another method, to the use of which half the charm of an old English cottage is due, that of building outshots. In the small house all that was needed was a row of posts parallel to the side of the house, from which rafters might be laid to the roof; the walls were then treated in a similar method to that used for the main walls of the house. By these additions the one-roomed cottage became a dwelling with several rooms, suitable for the small farm. The main apartment was called the house-part and had a buttery and possibly other chambers opening from it; afterwards a woman's part was added.

The earlier one-roomed cottage had no more than one storey, and that in no way ceiled. Stories are still told in the writer's village of a certain farm in Crimscot where the men slept in an unceiled room and rats fell through the thatch upon the beds; indeed there are still unceiled bedrooms in some Warwickshire villages. Upper rooms were for a long period built only over the smaller down-stair chambers, the house-part remaining open to the roof. When there was an upper room the approach was made by a simple ladder, in time supplanted by a stair, made of an inclined plane with rough triangular chunks of wood, pegged to it to form rude steps; such steps may be found sometimes beneath a modern stair. One may assume that the cottage of the period we are dealing with consisted of a woman's room, a hall, a buttery, and bed-rooms above the first and last.

The next development in the farm-house, as distinct from the cottage, is the union of the ox-stalls or skippon with the farmer's dwelling. In its simplest form it was but a cottage with a houseplace, buttery, and room above; it was approached by the usual ladder, but it had a large room adjoining, divided into aisles, and a root supported upon stone-based columns.

This formed a fodder store on one side, and had a row of ox-stalls on the other. In timber districts all the barns, ox-stalls, cow hovels, etc., were constructed in bays and built on crucks, but even when gavel forks were discarded the walls were of very slight height compared with the enormous roof. In stone districts where timber is scarce, stone was used as far as possible in houses and barn construction, but the system of bays was preserved everywhere, and buildings were described in terms of bays—a house of four bays, etc., and even the barns, etc., were reckoned in terms of bays.

In large farm and small manor houses the skippon was even more extended, and the central aisle was used for the storage of waggons and fodder. The house-part was at the further end, with the hall and bower of the master and the sleeping rooms of his family. The men-servants of the farm slept above the oxen, the milk-maids over the cows.

Farm-houses and cottages in the wooded districts were either timbered or half-timbered; in the former the whole framework of the house was of timber, in the latter the lower storey was stone-built. As a rule the older houses in the country had storeys which projected but slightly over the lower; when this was the case it was probably a utilitarian and not an artistic idea, the object being to prevent the roof drippings from sapping the foundations, or rotting the long groundsill from which the framework of the house arose. It may be added that the humbler and less pretentious houses were not meant to expose their timber work; they were very generally plastered over, and to assist the adhering power of the plaster were roughly notched with an axe, the tool by which the same timbers were rudely hacked out of the parent tree.

Occasionally the taste of the builder may be seen in carved brackets supporting timbers treated in conventional designs, and the gables adorned with an open-work barge board and pierced finial, which latter was duly copied in the stone-built house.

Methods of warming and lighting the house must now be considered, especially as many errors have surrounded this part of the subject.

About the household hearth gathered many relics of primitive religion. It was the shrine and centre of family life. Therein dwelt the Fire God, and to him offerings of ale and cake were nightly made. To her new home the bride brought a portion of fire from her mother's hearth, and had a fire been allowed to die out the result would have been disastrous. One must remember that on the open hearth wood and turf would have been used, and no other fuel, except in such favoured spots as possessed mines of sea-coal. The Warwickshire coal was used for fuel as early as the thirteenth century, if not much earlier.

In the early huts the fire was lighted in the centre, both for convenience and for divine protection; the smoke escaped as best it could. The method adopted in the early English homes to obviate this difficulty was the use of hoods of light timber and clay affixed to the side walls and shut in on three sides, of which the wall formed one, the door-screen another. The screen was itself furnished with a bench or seat in its inner side, and became converted into the chimney corner of the early days of the nineteenth century.

The hearth was always flat, of a large stone or brick work; on one side stood the settle, on the other the salt-box containing the household's supply of salt, which is even now brought round the villages by pedlars from Droitwich. This salt-box often had a small compartment in which the money of the owner was placed. On the flat hearth stood a pair of fire-dogs, and a steel fork was often present to handle the logs with. Sometimes a small window of a single pane of glass was placed in the nook, and the old stone oven was almost invariably built closely adjoining it.

Chimneys began to be part of walling of houses in the

early Middle Ages, and this necessitated the removal of the fire to the side walls, although chimney stacks in the centre of buildings are to be found.   The plan followed in cottages and farms was a wasteful one, since three walls of the chimney were exposed to the outside air. They were generally enormous excrescences in the centre of the gable, very large at the ground level and gradually narrowing.   They were swept, in later times at any rate, by boys kept for the purpose by the itinerant chimney-sweep, and often subjected to great cruelty and hardship. They were always supposed to flourish their broom outside the chimney pot and cry " Sweep."

The gradual inclination of the chimney upwards gave an opportunity of squaring and using the spaces around them—whenever, that is, they were built within a house ; such spaces frequently placed behind the stack made a dry and airy place for the preservation of bacon-sides, and incidentally have given rise to more than one bogus legend of priests' hiding holes, and, when the spaces were similarly used in the upper rooms, stories of ghosts laid within them have at times gained currency.

The accessories of the low hearth were simple in character and few in number ; across the open chimney just beyond reach of the flames a moveable gay-pole was placed at a slight angle, so that the iron-toothed rack from which a hook was suspended might be readily moved to one side from the flame.   The rack and hook were so arranged that the handle of the kettle or potato-pot could be held at the proper distance above the fire. Potato-pots are of great antiquity, and were used for most purposes of cooking.   They are circular in form, standing on three legs, or at other times have no feet. They were either suspended from the rack or stood on the hearth floor, and are the metal successors of the earthen cooking-pot of the cave and pit dwellers.   Skillets had usually long handles, three feet, and a small lip, to render it easier to empty out their liquid contents. The fondness for inscriptions among the good folk of these islands is borne out by these cooking vessels.   One in the British Museum is inscribed "Pity the Pore, 1684," and on another the patriotic words "Loyal to his Magiste." Kettles are of more recent introduction.

In addition to the rack, a moveable bracket known as a "sway" was much in evidence, and in elaborate specimens was so constructed that an adjustment to the fire was worked by a lever, so that the pot or kettle could be conveniently raised or lowered.

The first improvement was the introduction of an oven above, below, or upon the hearth. Such ovens, constructed of iron, are still in use in some of the farmhouses. It was only important farms or mansions that could boast of smoke jacks, or furnaces furnished with spits. The latter were the simpler. A system of iron bars ran in front of the fire, and on either side brackets to carry the long spit could be drawn out when required. The meat was then turned by hand, or in the case of the smoke jack by a fan placed in the chimney and set in motion by the upward draught. The drum of the fan was connected by a chain with the spit. A fine specimen exists at Aston Hall.

The chambers of the small farm or cottage were often lighted by window openings, over which a moveable frame, covered with cloth or canvas, was stretched. The cost of glass was too great for its use in private houses. Moreover, perhaps from this custom glass casements were removed and classed as personal property, so that the glazed windows did not of necessity pass to the next owner.

Windows were invariably glazed until recent times with lozenge-shaped panes, called "quarries," and these were framed in lead. Some of the quarries in the larger houses were ornamental and painted with a flower, the cypher of the owner, or a badge.

These do not, however, greatly concern us, since they would never be found in small cottages or farms. The old glass is greenish or yellowish in tint, and the rough bulb left in casting is often utilized, and sometimes an entire window will be made up of such panes.

Bottle glass gives a poor light, but it is not inartistic. In some situations where ventilation was necessary quarries were replaced by similar shaped panes in cast lead ; some of these are of excellent design. These fell into disuse with the introduction of perforated zinc.

The walls both inside and out were not left unadorned, but were coloured with a hard bright blue called " archil " derived from liverworts, a bright yellow ochre, or a wash of umber, and this not only on the inside but on the outside, where at times the timbered houses were painted with a brilliant blue or red. Occasionally on drab walls a band of navy-blue may be found with large spots of the same colour on either side. This looks like a painted imitation of a row of poles and wickerwork. A decided advance was made when the whole wall surface was stencilled with sprigs of green leaves, just as the cottage windows are dressed at Christmas with sprays of holly, or, as in the old church custom, set upright in the corners of pews. This idea of walls powdered with sprays gave rise to the earlier wallpaper designs. It is worth noting that in some Warwickshire estates the cottagers until toward the third quarter of last century were not allowed to paper their rooms, but had to content themselves with colour washes ; whether in obedience to old tradition or for sanitary reasons is not easy to say. The lime washing of the exterior was thought to be a preventive of fire. If blue it appeased divine wrath.

Ancient cottages were floored with either marl or clay beaten hard, and upon this straw or rushes were strewn. In stone districts floors were pitched either with flat stones or cobbles, which in due course were replaced by flagstones. A wooden floor was unknown. In Wimpstone one old cottage has a pleasing floor, made of alternate squares of lias and cobbles. This has been patched in places with malt kiln tiles, so that almost all dates and methods of flooring are represented.

Flagged floors were decorated with, apparently, unmeaning scribblings made by the rubbing-stone after cleaning. The idea is extremely old, as such markings were found in a hearthstone in Glastonbury Lake village, and its origin was probably religious. Some of the marks made to-day are mere twisted flourishes in the centre and round the edge of the stones, but it does not require any great effort of the imagination to see in them the survivals of the intertwined zoomorphs so characteristic of the eleventh century. Other forms of stoning draw a rude circle in the centre of the stone and an edge of circles about its sides; in another form looped lines are drawn across the diagonals of the stone from angle to angle, forming a saltire of St. Andrew's cross; in others again a series of lozenges occur, or rows of double loops. In the simplest form of all, the edges are surrounded by broad whited lines. That they are traditional there can be no doubt, and certain families keep to one particular pattern. A woman will say, " that is how my mother or grandmother did it."

When one remembers the sacred regard for the hearth and threshold among our primitive tribes, it is surely not too far-fetched to suggest a religious origin and connect them with fire and snake worship. There is even now a certain dislike to treading on a neighbour's threshold stone, and actions at law and pleas of trespass for this cause have arisen even in the twentieth century in the writer's village.

Before leaving this section it will be well to speak of the methods of obtaining a fire and light, and of the omens arising from them, before passing on to consider the scanty furniture and domestic utensils needed for the rough and simple lives led by the farmer of old days and his men.

Throughout the Middle Ages light was obtained from the ignition of tinder, i.e., burnt linen, kept in a box called a " tinder-box." A spark was struck from a suitable piece of flint by an iron or steel hook held in the hand. The spark falling on the tinder was gently coaxed into a flame by breath from the mouth, a process continued until living memory. An old man in the writer's parish remembers the language, more forcible than polite, when his father failed to obtain the needed light as rapidly as he desired.

From the fourteenth century, wooden sticks dipped in sulphur were used to apply to the flame raised in the tinder box. In living memory such matches were hawked about the villages in small boxes costing twopence-half-penny each by special purveyors of such ware. Friction matches did not come into use until about 1830, and were probably long in finding their way into the country. The light once applied, it did not invariably follow that the fire burnt up well and cheerfully. If it did it was customary to say "Your sweetheart is smiling" or an older parlance, "The fire is all a glee."

After dark the only method of lighting the house in common vogue was the rushlight, made of a wick of peeled rushes dipped in fat. The light given was a very feeble one. As an elderly man once said to the writer, "You had to light one to see the other."

When lighted they were set in any convenient holder— a hole bored in a square of wood, an old bottle, or a rush-light stand made of an iron holder set upright in a piece of wood.

A more complex apparatus was used in the larger houses. A drum of iron, pierced with circular holes some inches high and fairly large in diameter, was set on the bedroom floor; as the rushlight burnt down the circles of light grew gradually larger, until to the fevered imagination of at least one child they seemed to be great human eyes staring at the inmate of the bed. In the houses of the great, waxlights in sconces wonderfully carved gave a beautiful and much more brilliant light.

The guttering of a rushlight was made use of by the villagers for foretelling events. If it assumed a twisted form it betokened death, and represented a shroud or a winding sheet; a glowing portion of wick was taken to foretell the approach of a stranger, and these two omens are generally believed in most parts of England.

The fire omens cannot in some cases be of any great

age. If on lighting it burns well it is believed to be lucky ; sunlight is generally believed to put it out if it is allowed to shine too brightly or too directly upon a freshly kindled fire.

Hollow bombs are occasionally propelled from the fire by a slight explosion of gas ; if they do not tinkle when shaken they are accounted coffins, and the person to whom they are directed will die. If when shaken there is a metallic sound someone will attain money boxes, and they are the harbingers of good luck.

CHAPTER XII.

Furniture.

The furniture and utensils of the medieval farm were of the simplest; china and glass were unknown, earthenware far from common if one may judge from the scarcity of their remains. Vessels of wood and leather played a very conspicuous part, but here again leather could have been little used by the cottager. Some farmhouse inventories that have come down to us describe but little furniture. Tables were either trestle or frame; in the former the top could be removed when the meal was done; in the latter it was a fixture. Chairs were scarce; the occupants of the top and bottom of the table board sat on frame stools, those at the sides on forms. A cupboard was not uncommon, fixed in the corner of the room, and in the eighteenth century a long-cased or grandfather's clock was to be found in most houses.

The cooking utensils—forks, pots, skillets, etc.—have already been dealt with, but in the eighteenth century candlesticks of brass, with spoons and skimmers of the same metal, began to appear, and pewter garnishes took the place of the service of treen of the older days. Nevertheless the square treen platter, with its circular hollow, and smaller receptacle for salt were still in use; a more advanced form was turned on the lathe and was in itself circular. The pewter garnish was the pride of the good housewife and was kept beautifully clean; there were large circular dishes and circular platters of various sizes, salts, tankards, pepper pots, etc., and also candlesticks. They were cleaned according to Warwickshire custom by scouring with elderberry leaves.

Above the fireplace was fixed a rack to carry the fowling-piece, and four stout hooks suspended a moveable wooden bacon rack from the ceiling. In the larger farms this bacon was hung near the hearth, sometimes in a special form of bacon cupboard.

Upstairs there was still simplicity, perhaps even greater than downstairs. The clothing of the owner was kept in a chest or coffer, usually of oak, often well and handsomely carved. The bed was a rough frame of wood, supporting on four uprights a tester, so arranged that curtains could be drawn around the sleeper on all four sides, although a richer house would have a wooden headpiece and handsomely carved front posts. The bed clothing consisted of a feather bed, apparently the most highly prized article in the house, since the gift of feather beds is referred to in nearly every will of the sixteenth and seventeenth centuries, and that among both the rich and the humbler members of the community. The bed was spread usually upon a rush mat such as one sees beneath effigies of the sixteenth century, and that was in itself spread upon a stretch of harden or hurden drawn tight by cords passing through holes in the bed frame.

Occasionally in the rude bedsteads of cottagers upright sticks were placed at intervals along the side frame of the bed, after the occupants had retired to rest, to prevent them falling out. Besides a feather bed, there were pillows stuffed with feathers and resting on a pillowbere—the article we call a bolster. " A payre of sheets, a payre of blankettes, and a coverlett " completed the bed covering.

Sheets were in South Warwickshire almost entirely home made, spun from flax growing in the village. In most parishes one finds some record of presentations at the manor court for the offence of washing flax in the stream. It is probable that blankets were also made at home from the wool of the sheep. A necessary part of the furniture of the home was a spinning wheel, of which there were at least two kinds, one large and one small.

CHAPTER XIII.

FARM-WORK.

The yearly round of toil began in Merry England on Plough Monday, the Monday following after Twelfth Day, from time immemorial a day of feasting and revelry. On that day a plough, decked with ribbons, was drawn with all ceremony through the village street by its young men, to the strains of pipe and tabor. The custom had a wide geographical range, but there is scarcely a trace preserved of its occurrence in Warwickshire. The late Mrs. Colborne remembered her grandfather speaking of the custom as it was carried out at Ettington in his youth, towards the end of the eighteenth century. He also remembered a more interesting custom observed there, which differs considerably in detail from other records. On that day, he said, it was customary for the farm-girls to race from the house to the nearest furrow, snatch up a clod of earth and scamper back again, chased by the plough-boys with their whips. If the girls reached the farm kitchen in time to stick a few feathers in the clod of earth before the boys could place their whips upon the kitchen table, then the boys lost their ration of plum pudding.

Some rather detailed account of the plough itself is hardly out of place, since it is such an important instrument, and one on which so much depends. The heavy land of Warwickshire needed the employment of " the great plough," drawn by its yoke of eight oxen, yoked in pairs on either side of the long plough-pole. A heavy wooden yoke rested on the shoulders of the animals, and from either end a bow of iron passed round their necks, keeping them firmly secured in the desired position; a long pole connected the three or four yokes.

Oxen were employed in this way until recently, and also used to draw a cart, a not uncommon sight in many towns. A hundred years since, horses were rarely used for ploughing; they were considered to need more care at the end of their day's work than the sturdier oxen. When the oxen were " unshet " at the end of the day, it was a delight to the children to ride home on their backs. The writer has witnessed a team of bulls used with the plough on a farm at Southacre in Norfolk.

The ox-pole gave rise to the standard rod, pole, or perch of our familiar tables, and the normal strip of the common fields measured forty such poles in length by four in width, making an acre.

At Pebworth the plough was known as " the long-arsed plough," a direct survival of the ancient long-tailed plough described by Fitzherbert as consisting of " a plough beame, the longe tre above, on which the plough is set; the shar-beame, the tre underneathe; the ploughe-shethe, a thyne piece of longe woode made of oke that is set fast in a morteys in the plough-beame and shar-beame ; the ploughe tayle, the shelbrede, the fenbrede, the thread made of thorne, the plough fote, the plough eare, the culture, the plough mel. The geare belongynge bowes, yokes, landes, stylkynges, wrethynges, and temes," which belonged to the ox harness.

The plough was used not only to cultivate the land, but to render that important work possible. In all parts of the country the curved ridges and furrows may be seen, which our forefathers of a very remote date—how remote can only be conjectured—used to serve the purpose of drainage. The undulating lines followed the uncor-rected course the plough naturally took, since a plough does not travel in a straight line of its own sweet will.

All the arable land of the township lay in acre and half-acre strips, arranged as the land best allowed, but always necessitating a headland at either end of the strip to allow the plough to turn, and these headlands were ploughed last of all. They form an important part of the description of land in early deeds, wherein the portion to change hand is described as lying between the land of A on the North, B on the South, with a headland abut-ting on the land of C, and the other by the King's way, or some similar formula.

It is obviously a truism that in every village there
were some too poor to afford a plough team of their own,
and there was often co-operation, several families sharing
a plough between them.   A wooden plough, not of very
ancient date, was found a few years back in a barn at Long
Compton, a village in which ancient tradition dies very
slowly.   It is preserved at Ann Hathaway's cottage in
Shottery with many other obsolete agricultural implements.

The plough oxen were broken in at Little Wolford
by the very effective process of yoking them to a heavy
log, such as an old gate post, and turning them loose to
tire themselves out.   An aged farmer at Quinton said
that the harness in his day was much the same as that
used for horses, except that the collars buckled at the top,
and the two straps and mullin were fastened between the
horns.

The directions given to guide the beasts with the voice
were :   "Au" (come nearer to the near (left) side) ;
"Eet" (go more to the off (right) side) ;   "Comming
gen" (turn to the near side) ; and "Gee gen" (turn to
the off side).

Here and there pieces of land are to be found which
do not fit into the general plan ; these gores and lynches
were too precious to be left uncultivated.   The hillside
lynches were formed by the plough making a furrow only
one way, that is, down hill, producing a terrace in hilly
country.   These lynches are remarkable objects, giving
a strange appearance to the uninitiated.

Ploughing for corn setting was followed by bean setting,
which took place as early in the year as the condition of
the land allowed.   When it was completed the men and
boys were feasted with the standard dainties of butcher's
meat and plum puddings.   At Long Marston and Pebworth the feast was known as the "whipt cat," and cheese
and cyder was provided by the farmer.   This is the only
local mention of the cruel custom of enclosing a cat in a
basket and whipping it to death, presumably as a sacrifice
to the corn spirit that the author has met with.

Custom decreed that four beans were placed in each

hole. The following scrap of doggerel which Thomas
Baldwin of Crimscot recited explains the reason :—

> One for the pigeon, one for the crow,
> One to perish, and one to grow.

Peas were sown broadcast, a matter of no little skill.
To quote Fitzherbert once more :—

> You must not sow if the land synge or cry, or make any
> noyse under thy fete. Put thy pees into thy hopper and take
> a brode thong of ledder or of garthe webbe of an ell longe, and
> fasten it to the endes of the hopper, and put it over thy head
> like a leyshe, and stande in the myddle of the lande where the
> sacke lyethe .... and set thy left foote before, and take a
> handfull of pees, and when thou takest up thy right foote then
> caste thy pees from the alle abrode, and whan thy lefte fote
> repeth take an other handful .... and so at every 11 paces
> .... so that thy fote and hande agree, and than ye shal sowe
> even, and in your castynge ye must open as well your fyngers
> as your hande, and the hyer and farther that ye caste your corne
> the better shall it sprede.

This description tallies exactly with the method of
sowing on the common fields of Crimscot eighty years
since, as handed down by the grandfathers of living men.

Corn-setting was followed by harrowing and weeding.
The harrow drawn by its oxen was made of " bulles " of
oak or ash, through which " shotes " of wood were
passed ; each bulle had six sharp pieces of iron called
" harrow-tynes," set somewhat of a slope forward, the
foremost shote bigger than the others. The horse
harrow had but five bulles and was smaller in every part.
An old rhyme ran—

> The ox is never loo
> Till he to harrow go.

When the corn was planted and harrowed, meadow-
mowing commenced. In this the women helped their
men folk, but they were paid but sixpence a day, half as
much as the men. The farmer gave the mowers a barrel
of beer to stimulate their efforts.

On the first day of meadow-mowing each man

received a posy from his wife or sweetheart, who pinned
it in the smock—a pretty custom of great antiquity.
The strips of meadow belonging to the different farms
were marked permanently either by merestones or marks
cut in the turf. These marks at Crimscot were the
parson's hat, a plain circle marking the rectorial glebe;
the pig-trough, a spit more or less resembling a stone
trough, for "Eddens farm"; a round hole for "Beman's
farm," and the spit for Jaques's farm.

The men came to their labour before dawn, and in
the dark had often to feel for the merestones with their
feet; each man's mathe was marked out by "doles,"
and to make a proper start the mower "ran a tread" as
a guide to mow by, lest by chance he overcut his mathe
and encroached on the grass of another farm.

Occasionally some grass lay outside the system; such
a plot was called "parting-grass," and was cut by the
fieldsman and made into a cock by itself and shared out
later to the owners.

The mowers occasionally cut into the corners called
"pikes," caused by odd angles where the lands met, and
disputes had in this case to be settled by arbitration.

At the completion of the task at Ilmington the last
few stems of uncut grass were twisted together so that
the flower spikes formed a rude imitation of a cock's
head; the mowers then stepped back and, after being
blindfolded, attempted to cut it with their scythes; failure
was punished by a fine of a quart of beer.

The squire gave to each man a shilling and each
woman sixpence, and his gamekeepers provided a barrel
of beer as an inducement to the mowers to avoid disturbing sitting partridges.

From the neighbourhood of Brailes hill come the
traces of what looks like the survival of the sacrifice to
the corn spirit. A cock was brought into the field and
fastened by a string to a stake, while the men stood at a
distance and shot at it, the lucky sportsman receiving the
bird as his reward. On one occasion the wily fowl was
too quick for his enemies, and dodged the shots until a

gamekeeper charged his piece with a silver sixpence. There is no such a tale told at Whitchurch, but the last strands of corn were knotted to represent a cock's head and thrown at with sickles. The meadow-mowing sometimes overlapped harvest, but in most seasons a short break intervened.

The chief feast of the year followed on the harvest; all the men, women and boys rode home on the last load, the horses' headstalls were gaily decorated with flowers, and horns were blown. Almost every village seems to have its own version of the harvest-home rhyme—

> Up! Up! Up! a merry harvest home,
> We have sowed, we have mowed,
> We have carried our last load

is general as at Wimpston, but at Aston Cantlow it ran—

> Up! Up! Up! for the harvest home,
> Three plum puddings and a bacon bone.

At Ilmington the second line ran, "A good plum pudding and a good beef bone."

Another of later date, after a bad harvest, breathes a certain discontent—

> Hip! Hip! Hip! for the harvest home.
> Now we've taken the last load home.
> I ripped my shirt and I teared my skin
> To get my master's harvest in.

With a very exceptionally bad year, and some years were terrible, the Wimpstone folk sang—

> The bread aint done, the cheese aint come,
> The Devil never knew such a harvest home.

At the supper boiled beef and carrots was the staple fare, taken from the pot in the old way with a flesh-fork; the second course was the inevitable plum pudding, and both were washed down with draughts of specially brewed ale. At the end the health of the master was sung. The words are quite usual and well enough known ; but at

Long Marston there is a notable addition, given in italics
below—

> Here's a health unto our master, the founder of the feast,
> *I hope to God in Heaven his soul may be at rest.*
> That all things may prosper whate'er he takes in hand,
> For we are all his servants, and all at his command.
> So drink, boys, drink and see you do not spill,
> For if you do you shall drink two
> For his our master's will.

The prayer for the master's soul is certainly not
modern.

The supper table at Ilmington was decorated with a
small sheaf and a wooden vessel shaped like a bushel,
full of ale.

At Armscot, on the return of the last load, the mistress met the wain with an offering of cakes and ale, while
the gates of the farm were set open. The driver himself
wore feminine garments.

After the harvest the women and children went
leasing* in the fields, the signal for the start being given
on a horn; the oldest woman told the others where to go,
and all wore clean petticoats on the first day.

The corn obtained was in part made into a diminutive
stack and kept in the best bedroom. The bulk was
winnowed by hand; a day was chosen when the wind was
sufficient but not too strong, a sheet was spread on the
ground, and the corn, previously beaten from the ear, cast
into the air, the wind carrying away the chaff.

The farmer's crop was of course threshed with the
flail, yet another of the clever implements invented by
early man, which, in spite of their apparent awkwardness,
are so perfectly adapted to their requirements. A flail
consisted of the flail proper, always made of crab-apple;
this, which was free to move in every direction, was fixed
by thongs of eel skin to a bent piece of wood, or later
iron, turning on an iron pin set in the handle or threshole.

The sheaves were laid out on the threshing floor in

---

* Known also as gleaning in other counties.

the barn—a floor made of puddled clay rammed hard—in such a manner that the ears of corn met. A skilled thresherman could bring down the strokes of his flail exactly in the right spot, each falling parallel to the last. The novice more often than not found the flail meet his head.

The crop, whether of corn or hay, was carted on a wain, which differs little to-day from the rude vehicle Fitzherbert knew. He says :—

The bodye was supplied with a cart ladder, the wheles had nathes, spokes, and fellyes and clowses, they should be well fettred with wood or yren, and if they be yren bounden they be moche better.

To load the wain " a copyoke, a payre of sleues, a wayne rope and a pykfork " were needed.

The cottager's wife used her barley leasings to make the malt she needed for her brewings. The barley was put to soak, then allowed to chit, and spread evenly on the warm floor of the oven ; to test the correct heat a small child was pushed in, at the risk of being half choked, poor mite. An ancient dame of ninety summers told me she had often had the unpleasant ordeal.

The breast plough is a cumbrous tool much used until in recent times in the Stratford-upon-Avon district. It is not exactly a rival to the plough, since it uses a human being as its driving force, and with naturally less effect. It is pushed along the ground and pares a slice from its surface, so that the stubble, weeds, and other rubbish can be raked up and burnt. Whole fields have been ploughed by this tool by a gang of men following one another. The plough has a broad triangular blade fastened to a stout pole with a cross handle at the end to enable the worker to push with both hands, his body being used to give more persistent and steadier impetus to the action. It is protected by two hollowed-out pieces of wood or leathern guards strapped over the thighs. The strain is very great and the work most laborious.

Land drainage is often necessary, indeed most farms

have wet parts needing attention. The most ancient and
simplest method has already been alluded to, but another
very old method is that of digging a trench and placing
thornboughs in it ; many years pass before the thorn
decays, and, so long as it lasts, water finds its way through
and the drainage is more or less satisfactory. Near
Shipston, in one case, old horns of the cattle killed in the
slaughter yards were put to the same use, the tips were
cut off and the horns inserted in each other, making some
sort of continuous drain, but the area affected could not
have been large.

The foremost of the farm servants was the shepherd.
His position made for great care and patient, not to say
at times unpleasant, work ; on him depended the increase
and well-being of the flock. He had his peculiar per-
quisites in the lambing season, among them that of a
pancake when the first lamb was announced.

Sheep are still distinguished as tegs, thaves, and
sharreves, while a couple is "a ewe and her lamb," and
a double couple "a ewe with her two lambs." The
restlessness of sheep is counted as a sign of bad weather,
and on one occasion a ram barketting about in a hedge
undoubtedly caused the writer to escape a wetting on a
cloudless June morning, or rather the warning of its
ancient guardian did. They may have been wrong, both
sheep and shepherd, but the rain came in a deluge,
as rain can come down in the Cotswolds. (In this connection see Br. ii., p. 243.)

The sheep-shearing feast was the great event of the
shepherd's year. All helpers on the farm took a part in it,
including the blacksmith and the visiting tailor ; even
these worthies essayed to shear some unfortunate victim.
Once upon a time the shearers had a posy in their smock
frocks, but the custom did not survive the early days of
last century. As a perquisite each man tied a piece of
wool round his shears when he finished work ; it hardly
looks worth his while, but a local saying runs : "a piece of
wool the size of a bee's knee will make a yarn as long as
a man's fingernail."

Yarn was spun at home on a jersey wheel, which was larger than the ordinary wheel, and from such yarn jersey stockings were knitted.

By ancient custom the shearing must take place with the increase of the moon. Its completion heralded in a great feast, with stuffed chine in the place of honour. Few are left who can stuff a chine as it was stuffed in the good old days; it was indeed a dish for the gods, washed down with cyder and home brewed, a fitting prelude to the dance which ended the day.

In early days in England none but the lord might have a sheep fold and be accounted foldworthy. It was a practical necessity he very thoroughly enforced—he needed the muck. His villeins had to be content with depasturing the herd and flocks on the common fields.

As the shepherd was a great man, so too was the cowherd and oxherd. They led the cattle to the field each day with a blast from a horn, at the sound of which each man's beasts came from the byre to join the herd, and from that moment until sunset they remained under his care. It was his duty to prevent their straying into another township or into the standing corn; he led them to water and a lairing hole at midday, and brought back the cows to be milked at eventide. His method of reckoning the time was simple : he set up a pole and watched how the shadow fell; if there was no sun the hour was guessed at.

One curious idea prevailed that geese, donkeys and goats, all non-commonable animals, were at times turned out with the cows to prevent them casting their calves.

Agriculture in England made slow improvement; one gathers this from the various treatises which appeared from time to time. The *Book of Husbandry*, 1534, says that cart-wheels were sometimes bound with iron, but the rival merits of horses and oxen for the plough were still in dispute; the roller was beginning to be used for barley crops and staddle stones coming into fashion. Tusser in 1562 knew of carrots, cabbages, turnips and rape, but only for kitchen use. Sir John Norden, in his

Surveyor's Dialogue, 1607, mentions clover as sown with other hay seeds. Sir Richard Weston, *Husbandry of Brabant*, 1645, speaks of clover and turnips grown as field crops abroad. In 1681 Houghton, *Collections on Husbandry*, suggests the use of turnips to feed sheep. Tull's *Horse-shoeing Industry*, 1731, shows that wheat drilling, introduced about 1701, was well established. The Society of Improvers, in their Transactions for 1745, notice a threshing machine invented by one Richard Menzies, worked by a wheel rotated by water.

CHAPTER XIV.

Occult Influences.

Village folk must have lived in an ever-present dread
of evil spells ; possibly the terrible picture of Hell and
its denizens, which adorned the walls of their little church
in all the crudity of rude painting, may have helped; in
any case, belief in a personal and very active devil and
his earthly helpers, witches, was seldom far from their
thoughts, and to one or both every mischance was
blamed.

Witchcraft still exists or is believed to do so, though
little is heard of it, nor is it wholly absurd or worse.
A supposed compact between an ugly and decrepit old
woman and the evil one seems to us mere cozenage ; but
these deluded people may well have desired power, and, if
they could not be loved, might well wish to be feared.
They are not the only folk in history that have sacrificed
much for the limelight. It may be that a hard and bitter
life gave them fuller knowledge of the inner working of
the human mind than their neighbours ; they had but to
add the muttering of a spell or the brewing of herbs and
simples to obtain a reputation for supernatural power.
Imagination did the rest. Some of them inherited the
secret traditional lore of the tribe, in which much that
was pagan survived. To the popular mind they laid
spells for good or ill, and were sought for many reasons,
for love, hate and revenge. At times they were cruelly
persecuted, the mob getting the better of their fears and
harrying these unfortunates to death. Did we but know
their secrets, which perished unwritten, modern science
might well be the gainer.

Black witches* were the avowed enemies of all good

* Br. iii. 4.

things, white witches befriended man, and grey took a middle path neither actively bad nor actively good.

The witch of the church's ban and the victim of the law was credited by a solemn compact with the Devil, always described as a man in black, to whom she surrendered her soul and body, and ratified the contract by a deed signed in her blood, confirmed by a coin received from her tempter to indicate complete sale. She then had a familiar spirit assigned to her, such as a black cat, who carried out her behests, and at times sucked her blood.*

The extreme south of Warwickshire was a stronghold of these creatures; they held their Sabbaths there,† at the Rollright stones, a megalithic circle, to which green lanes converge along the hill tops, and in Stone-Age days a mighty temple to the sun.

The circle lies actually in Oxfordshire. It is only about 100 feet in diameter and formed of 70 stones. An upright monolith, the Kingstone, stands apart from the rest. A third group known as the "Whispering Knights" is at some distance to the east. The hill on which the circle stands is about 700 feet above sea-level.

Naturally a story arose to account for such a rare arrangement, and it is still told by the cottage fire. A pagan king heard tell that if he and his knights and men climbed the hill till they could see Long Compton church, then the crown of England would be his.

The action of a witch, to whom the name of Mother Shipton is now given, prevented the expected reward. Her words—

> Rise up hill, stand still stone,
> King of England thou shall be none

with appropriate charms, sufficed. Whereupon the King, his knights and their followers were turned into these stones, which still witness their fate.

---

* Br. iii. 6.   † Br. iii. 8.

The following lines have been in print probably more than once, but seem worthy of a place here :—

> She stood upon Long Compton hill
> And glared upon the vale.
> Ere to-morrow's height,
> I'll blast the might
> Of King and men in mail.
> I spy them in the burra,
> But me they cannot spy;
> The King before,
> The men two score,
> I'll blast them with mine eye.
> They shall not reach the hill-top,
> Long Com. they ne'er shall see,
> For with that sight
> Is gained the right
> Old England's King to be.
> Here on the windy headland
> I'll freeze them all to stones,
> My cruel spell,
> And trick of Hell,
> Shall turn to flint their bones.
> All round the ruddy flare
> They sit and sip and sing,
> "Tomorrow we
> Long Com. shall see
> And crown great England's King."
> They leave to you her den hard by,
> Their vain burst heard with glee,
> And clutching in her shrivelled hand
> She stirred the deadly pottage
> And muttered horribly.

A young farmer living in his hillside farm said sorrowfully that he could not keep any gate shut on the way to the stones, nothing he could think of, not even new padlocks, were any use at all ; all would be secure at night, but in the morning the gates were found open and the cattle astray. Naturally the witches were to blame.

Another said that his father, wanting to bridge a culvert near the house, tried to draw one of the stones down the hill. It was very difficult work and his team were all in a malt sweat, as if terrified. The team had to be unharnessed, it was thought well to take the stone back ; this a single horse managed quite easily.

The following letter received in answer to certain inquiries from Mr. J. S. is of interest in this connection :—

I have made a few inquiries regarding the witch-lore of the district, and according to my information Jenny R . . . . was the Blackwell witch, Darscot boasting the possession of a compeer in Betty H . . . . In her time my grandfather and grandmother lived at Darlingscot, occupying the farm now tenanted by Mr. Rainbow. Betty lived with her husband, a quiet inoffensive old chap, in an adjacent cottage, and I have complete proof that my relatives fully believed in her supernatural power. My grandmother had sometimes given Betty articles of clothing, etc., but at length she became so bold and intrusive that she was forbidden the premises. After this various annoyances came. The butter would not come, the cheese was a failure, or the fire would not burn. These things were all put down to the account of Betty. It was commonly held that a witch had power over a person of whom she had received gifts. If anything went wrong my grandmother would say, " Oh, it's old Betty H., I know she's got a hank on me."

Betty sometimes assumed the form of a hare, especially during her night rambles. The men of the village made resolute efforts to shoot the witch-hare, but it seemed to have a charmed life. Once, however, it was wounded, and sure enough Betty was laid up with a gammy leg.

It is said that farmers returning from Stratford market at night were often held up by an invisible something at Bruton barn near Ilmington ; their horses would not pass the spot, sometimes for an hour or more. This was supposed to be Betty's work.* I can imagine that the belated market-peart farmers of that period would work this excuse for all it was worth. " Got stopped by the witch agen me wench " he would reply to the sharp questioning of his ruffled spouse.

---

* Miss J. of Wimpstone gave another reason, viz., that the stoppages were due to a burial of a highwayman at the cross-roads, where he was interred with a stake through his belly. This man is more likely to have been some unfortunate under the ban of the greater excommunication.

But it is extremely improbable, I think, that the witchery which proved so potent was always received at the Bruton turn. Even superstition it seems had its good points as an excuse.

My aunt tells me that my grandfather really believed that he once encountered Betty in the following curious circumstances: One night a terrific thunderstorm was raging, and he and the carter went to fetch in the horses which were "at tie" in the fields, fearing that the animals might take fright and hurt themselves. They were leading the horses away when suddenly something rushed past the head of the foremost. It was Betty riding full tilt on a hurdle. The carter was fully occupied holding the plunging horses, and so was unable to observe Betty at close quarters, but my grandfather said he never saw her plainer in his life. He tried to point out the witch as she vanished, but the carter never saw her. "Can't you see her?" he said, "yonder her goes; up and down, ridge and furrow."

With reference to witches, my grandmother had a servant girl from Newbold whose grandmother was a reputed witch. The girl spoke of mysterious noises issuing from her clothes-box at night which alarmed her. Once a table full of crockery-ware was upset in the kitchen, but the girl avowed that she never touched it. Curiously enough nothing was broken. The girl believed that her grandmother had a hank on her.

Mrs. F .... of Long Compton could assume at will any form she chose to take, but always white; she might be a mouse, a cat or a rabbit, but white was always her colour. On one occasion, while in the form of a rabbit, she was accidentally run over, and had her arm in a bandage the next day. Who can gainsay such evidence? In the same village lived another Mrs. F., a midwife, who, called up one night to attend a case, was flung from the path by the roadside into a ditch by a white cat she had struck with her umbrella; helping herself out of the water and mud as best she could, the poor woman found she had lost one of her pattens, but discovered it dancing down the road. This rough treatment was attributed to the professional jealousy of a certain Mrs. Ann H .... n.

Old Mrs. H .... s was so sadly bewitched that she could not die while her relatives were present, so at her entreaty both they and her neighbours left the room. At once there arose a terrible tumult; on rushing in they found her possessions strewn about and her boxes and chest of drawers turned inside out in dire confusion. A black pigeon flew out of the window—the old lady was dead.

Another tale runs that a young man of the same parish sold himself to the evil one in the Close; this is a field near the church with the remains of early earthworks, just the spot for such a scene.

In the centre where the paths crossed he drew the semblance of a circle and read the Lord's Prayer backwards; after the compact, sealed as usual with his blood, he was assigned twelve imps as his familiars and servants. One of his exploits was at Banbury Fair, where he raised the evil one in the form of a black cock.

Another local lady, Mary W ...., put Henry Jeffs under "an ill tongue," but old John Wheeler, the then schoolmaster, took some parings from his finger and toe-nails, put them in a stone jar, then "hotted the oven as hot again as if for baking; they done it in the night and sealed em over." This queer proceeding is said to have caused such pain to the witch that she removed the spell.

All these stories were seriously told, after much persuasion and with some fear of the consequences, in 1912. They rather lend point to the saying, " There are enough witches in Long Compton to draw a waggon load of hay up Long Compton hill." Very similar stories were current both at Brailes and Tysoe, and probably in most if not all villages in the days of our forefathers.

In 1875 a weak-minded young man killed an old woman named Ann Turner with a hay-fork because he believed she had bewitched him. At the trial he begged she might be weighed against the church bible. This is the only local reference to this well-known practice.

The halfway house between the villages of Tredington and Honington was the haunt of Betty P . . . . t, well known to be one of the sisterhood. In her life she frequented a withy tree, at the top of which she would sit pulling on her stockings ; after her death she haunted the wall of the church, where she was seen smoking a pipe.

Another Tredington woman, old Betty L . . . . s, caused a good deal of trouble to her neighbours. One of them had a friendly party in his cottage, but neglected to invite Betty. She came in the form of "sumot like a cat," but was detected and wounded in the right paw by a man with a pitchfork ; puss disappeared through the keyhole, and in the morning the poor woman was found suffering from a wound in her right hand, which never properly healed.* This same woman had a grudge against a farmer named Lambley, and laid a spell upon him so that he could not get a fire to light nor the beer to brew ; his butter refused to come, no matter how long the churn was turned, even the cow would not pass down the lane to be milked. A timely weekly present of milk saved any more annoyance.

A certain old inhabitant of Wimpstone, George Bailey, a man of considerable intelligence, knew a woman carrier between Audley and Coventry whose will power must have been great. She told him she would convince him that her power was a real one. He chanced to go to her house on business one miserable snowy day in mid-winter. She said she would fetch her sister for him. This woman lived in a cottage ten miles away. She then took twelve new pins,† thrust them into an apple and muttered some charm he could not catch, and put the apple in the fire. About noon her sister walked in saying that something she could not resist seemed to force her to come.

There is an old story from Warwick Castle which is too good to be omitted, since it is certainly of very respectable antiquity. Something very similar may be found in the pages of Rous. The more modern version

* Br. iii. 15. † Br. iii. 13.

H

has gathered to itself some of the older details. As now told it runs thus :—

An old retainer named Moll Bloxham was allowed to sell for her own gain some of the superfluous milk and butter not needed by the family. She lived in a cottage hard by the walls and was supposed to cheat her customers sorely, following the old rhyme—

> Milk and butter I sell ever,
> Weight and measure I give never.

After a long period of grace these practices reached the ears of the Earl, and the supply was cut off. In revenge the old lady haunted the castle in the form of a black dog. The combined efforts of three of the clergy of the town to exorcise the spirit was unavailing for a time, but at last she sprang from Cæsar's Tower into the river below, and was imprisoned within a chamber contrived beneath the fletcher dam. Her statue was placed on the tower to mark the spot from whence she leapt to her doom.*

In Willington in 1880 a servant girl lifted a spell laid on her cows by taking a cow's heart, sticking it with pins and roasting it in the oven—by which means the witch in one of her transformations would be drawn there. In this case a small animal, "the like of which none of them had ever seen, came and scratted at the stopless closing the oven door, trying to reach the heart." The death of this creature ended the spell. The grandson of the said clever young woman was responsible for the tale, which is quite of the usual type.

Yet more extraordinary is the story of Nance A . . . . of Brailes, who, besides appearing when she wished as a white cat or rabbit, baked for her neighbours, and then, if she was hostile to her friends, put a spell on the oven so that the door would not open. She was credited with the power of suspending girls from the ceiling by the

---

* This statue was obviously that of a "watcher," with which the castle towers of the period were supplied, that an enemy, trusting to surprise the sleeping garrison, might think a sentinel was watching them from the ramparts.

hair, and making them walk on it like flies. This was believed in 1914.

The story told of the battle of Kineton, fought October 2nd, 1642, the first serious engagement of the Civil War, is still told in the vicinity, much as it was told at the time in a rare tract. The modern version, and it is oral tradition we are chiefly concerned with, runs thus :—

A wounded soldier left on the field found himself able to crawl about and in a ghoulish manner rob the dead, then he made his way to a tavern at no great distance, where he obtained lodging, and gave his ill-gotten gains to the landlord and his wife to take care of. When well enough to leave he asked for it to be returned to him, and both denied that he ever gave them any. In due course he brought an action at law, and the Devil appeared to him at night offering to assist him in return for his soul. This was further than the man was willing to go, but the tempter said he would assist him all the same. He said he would be present at the trial wearing a red cap. Among the jurors a man in such a cap duly appeared. The landlord swore he had never received any money from his lodger, adding that he hoped the Devil would take him if he had. Whereupon the red-capped juryman sprang up, threw the perjurer over his shoulder and disappeared. The story does not say what became of the soldier. The moral is rather hard to see, for that creature scarcely deserved much consideration.

Ghost stories are not very common in the neighbourhood of Stratford-upon-Avon, and very few of those told have any particular interest. The countryside abounds with stories of a coach drawn by headless horses and driven by a coachman similarly inconvenienced. Such a tale is told of Harrow Hill in Long Compton and of Pig Lane in Ilmington. In the latter case the coach was supposed to contain a local magnate, who, in a fit of temper, had murdered a neighbour, and only visited his home at dead of night.

At Ilmington one Edward Golding, the parish clerk, who died in 1793, haunted the church long after his death, walking up and down at night muttering the responses, as he did in his lifetime.

At Alveston a plough lad named Charles Walton met a dog on his way home nine times in successive evenings. He told both the shepherd and carter with whom he worked, and was laughed at for his pains. On the ninth encounter a headless lady rustled past him in a silk dress, and on the next day he heard of his sister's death.

Hilborough Lane was haunted by a ghostly carriage and pair, and the field hard by the spot by a lady in white with a phantom stag of the same colour. No one coming from Bidford would pass Hilborough after nightfall.

Ragley Park adds to the list the tale of a lady in white, who appeared to many people after nightfall in a certain spot. Here it is said the skeleton of a woman was found, fully dressed and decked with beautiful jewelry.

For generations Alscot has produced stories of a ghost, half calf, half man, supposed to haunt both the park and the neighbouring lanes. In the writer's personal experience uncanny things do happen at night in the darkness of a deer park. One has the unpleasant sense of being dogged by something one cannot see and hardly hear. If, as at Alscot, a white-faced doe manages to escape, it is easy to see how its appearance in the gap of a hedge in the faint moonlight might easily suggest to the rustic mind a half human form. The inhabitants of Wimpstone were far too frightened to go down their lane when this particular doe or ghost was at large.

This belief in the occult has given rise to terrible cruelty both in England and abroad, and some of the worst cases of the legal outcome of superstitious fear must be noticed. The bull of Pope Innocent III. published in 1484 brought thousands of innocent people to the stake, while a great number of others, mostly old and decrepit women, perished from the tests applied. In England the statute of the 33rd of Henry VIII. (1541) made witchcraft a felony, and its decrees were again promulgated in that of the 5th of Elizabeth (1562) and the 1st of James I. (1603). The King himself was

very bitter against witches and sorcerers in his *Dæmono-
logie* published in Edinburgh in 1597. It may be well
to remember that the 73rd canon of the Church of
England, 1603, prohibits the clergy from casting out
devils. Far better known are the nefarious persecutions
brought about by the witch-finder, Mathew Hopkins,
who brought to their death between 1645—7 at least
100 wretched old women in Essex, Norfolk and Suffolk.
Two witches were burnt alive by order of Sir Mathew
Hale in 1664. In the adjacent county of Northampton
two were executed in 1705 and five others soon afterwards, while at Huntingdon in 1716 a Mrs. Hicks and
her daughter, aged nine, were hung. It is said that
nearly 2000 persons must have perished in England
under these various legal enactments. What a ghastly
mistake and travesty of religion !

CHAPTER XV.

Fairs and Markets.

The one means that country folk had in early times
of obtaining goods and chattels their immediate neighbourhood could not supply lay in the opportunity the
annual wake or fair provided, though a variety of things
were afterwards sold in the weekly market.

Fairs originated in very remote times among our
Teuton progenitors, and were by them associated with
their Temple worship. On such occasions national
sacrifices were offered and the assemblies of the folk
held; booths of green boughs were erected round about
the sacred enclosure, and the populace enjoyed themselves
after their manner. Such festivals were held at the
solstices and at the end of harvest. The year began
within the Yule feast; another feast was that in September, when thanks for the ingathered crops were
offered and sacrifices made to secure a prosperous winter.
There were other important festivities in November.

The fairs and wakes familiar to us were almost always
held on the feast of the patron saint of the church. In
this connection it is as well to remember the letter
Gregory the Great wrote to bishop Mellitus in 601,
urging that some solemnities must be provided for the
English people that they may build themselves booths
from boughs of trees about those churches which have
been turned to Christian use. Such gatherings were not
entirely religious, or for amusement, as business was
conveniently carried on where so many were assembled
together. On these occasions a special truce called " the
peace of the fair " obtained. It is referred to in Domesday Book under Dover. They had the protection of the
King's peace, so that men might assemble and depart to
their homes molested by no man. Legally all fairs were
classed as markets, but, on the other hand, Coke says all
markets were not fairs; indeed, there is a fundamental

distinction. Fairs were held only once a year, markets at closely recurring intervals. They were not primarily established for pleasure, but for trade purposes, and tolls were charged, which were a very valuable franchise. Many markets as early as Domesday paid toll to the Crown. No new market could be established, according to Bracton,* within six and two-thirds of a mile of another or to the detriment of the interests of the Crown. This curious distance was thus arrived at. A day's walk was reckoned at 20 miles ; a third of a man's time would be spent reaching the market. The middle of the day would be occupied with his business, and he could return home before nightfall, when the roads were no longer safe.

Distinction was already made as early as the reign of King John between a fair and a wake. The fair of Sallingeford was in dispute ; the abbot to whom it belonged pleaded that it was not a fair but a wake, which he and his ancestors had held from time immemorial, and that without paying toll. Eventually fairs could only be granted by royal charter, but far the majority of English fairs were held by ancient custom, and had no written record to prove by whom they were originally instituted. The oldest Warwickshire fairs able to show their charter are those of Coleshill in 1207-8 ; Brinklow, 1217-18 ; Bidford, both the market and fair, granted 1219-20 ; Nuneaton, both, in 1225-6 ; Kineton, both, in 1229-30 ; Stratford in 1239-40, and Warwick market in 1225.

The fair ground was removed from the churchyard owing to abuse under the Statute of Winchester (13 Edward I., cap. 6), but a case is recorded† where the churchwardens of St. Laurence's in Reading leased a stand in the church porch at fayer time in the year 1499 for 4d., but church porches were used for many things other than the purpose for which they were built.

To take the small fairs and wakes first. The barbarous sport of shin-kicking seems to have been general. Contests were engaged in for belts, and a month before the

_____

* *De legibus,* f. 235.   † Br. ii.

event the would-be victors rubbed their shins with blue vitriol to harden them. They wore special boots, the leather of which was dressed with the same chemical. On the appointed day the challenger threw his hat into the ring and his opponent did the same ; the pair then went at it fiercely, and a broken leg was not uncommonly the result.

The wake at Newbold-on-Stour was held on the feast of SS. Philip and James (May 1), that at Preston-on-Stour at the old thatched tavern in that village. It lasted from Saturday to Monday after the first Sunday in May—the usual sports of bowling and wrestling combined as usual with heavy drinking, and the custom of dancing for a piece of print for a frock, vigorously contested by the women folk. A stall for sweets was the sole survival in recent years, and even this has gone. In the old days Ilmington supplied the fiddler.

Alderminster wake was held on the Saturday before Whitsunday and lasted for a week. On Monday the men played bowls for a leg of mutton, Tuesday was given up to dancing, on Wednesday the women played bowls for a currant cake, and adjourned to the " Bell " for dancing and imbibing ; if a man came into the inn parlour he was seized by the women and kept in duress until he paid 6d. fine. One Betty Rose was the most accomplished dancer. At Bearley the wake began on Whitsunday at the inn known as " Bearley Cross." It lasted two or three days, and was followed by Snitterfield. Quinton also had a wake beginning on Whitsunday, while Tredington people held theirs on June 28th, the feast of St. Agatha. The fiddler, named Penn, came from Stretton. Shottery wake was held the first Tuesday in July, Aston Cantlow on the second Sunday in that month ; it lasted a week. Whatcot on the 11th of July (St. Benedict's Day), Ettington about the 18th. Of these the fair of Aston Cantlow was the most important ; various races were a leading feature, with donkeys, wheel-barrows, and in sacks, and at an earlier day sword-play and wrestling. The sword-players were not reckoned of much account until blood was drawn. Men and women danced all night. The neighbouring gentry and farmers attended the bowling matches. Ilmington wake was held at the "Fox" on the second Sunday in October, and was largely patronized to see the badger baiting, since Ilmington dogs were in high repute for their courage. There are plenty of badgers still in the dense thorn brakes of the neighbourhood. Mr. Samuel Bennett told the writer he had many times handled them with his naked hands, and often been severely bitten. It was the custom to put the dogs into the holes backwards. This was a feature also at a wake held on Meon Hill, probably very ancient, but the date seems to have slipped from living memory.

This allusion to Meon Hill, which is a curious semi-detached member of the Cotswolds, reminds one of the many curious legends which gather round it. The crest of the hill is the site of a late Stone-Age camp, and is studded with pit-dwellings. Within its ambit some Celtic chief of the Bronze-Age period left his hoard of treasure, some 300 currency bars, specimens of which may be seen at Stratford. These came from Honington Hall, where the writer bought what was left of the rusty remains.

The hill itself was formed by the evil one himself, in a fit of extreme annoyance caused by the building of Evesham Abbey by St. Ecguuine. He gave a violent kick as he sat and watched the distant edifice from Ilmington Hill. He hoped to overwhelm the whole—the Saint, his monks, and the abbey, but St. Ecguuine was watching, and prayer prevailed ; the hill merely fell where it now is. Another version runs that he kicked a large stone at the abbey, but it only reached the hill above Cleeve Prior, and the inhabitants there, to prevent any such wicked use in the future, made it the base of a cross, and there it stands to this day to prove the truth of the story.

Along the villages of the plain below the hill are many old folk living who will tell to those they can trust creepy stories of the Hell-hounds, Night-hounds, or Hooter, as they are variously named, that in phantom wise, with hounds and horn, pursue phantom foxes along the hill-tops at midnight. Many are the legends to account for uncouth sounds at night, which certainly do occur. One story is told of a local huntsman who would not desist from his favourite sport even on the Sabbath. On one Sunday judgment fell upon the ungodly crew ; huntsmen, horses, and hounds fell into a chasm that opened in the hill and were never seen again, though they still in ghostly wise hunt at midnight. F. S. P. recorded that an Ilmington yeoman, whose love for the chase became his absorbing passion, kept a pack of harriers of his own. One night his hounds seemed panic-stricken, and to quiet them he went out to their kennels in his night attire ; unfortunately they did not recognize their master, but tore him to pieces. He still hunts them on Xmas Eve and New Year's Eve, and woe to any person opening a gate or obeying a command of the ghostly huntsman, as they can then be carried off by him to their eternal destruction.

Of far greater importance are those fairs which had a legal standing as created by statute. Of such are the Mopps or Michaelmas fairs. One such was held at Shipston and another at Stratford. This latter sixty years since was quite a small affair, but it has grown to an unwieldy size owing to the popularity of the roasted pigs and bulls supplied to the thronging sight-seers. At Stratford the beast—there was then but one—was roasted whole in the street before the Garrick Inn. The money for the animal and the necessary expenses was collected from the public by the borough constable, who superintended the process in his own august person and collected payment for the plates of meat sold. The fair was at first confined to the inhabitants of the town, but other villages gradually joined in, and other publicans and cookshop proprietors roasted carcases of their own as a good investment, and now the shows and stalls spread over Bridge Street, Wood Street and Rother Street, and even

further. Like other fairs of its class it was instituted for
the hiring of farm servants of both sexes, who were hired
at it for a year and a day. The men and women awaiting
a master fastened in their clothing or head-dress a badge
of the service they wished to undertake. A groom
carried a bit of sponge and a brightly coloured whip,
a day labourer a wisp of plaited hay, a shepherd a lock of
wool. It is now a purely pleasure affair, bringing crowds
of visitors from Birmingham and other towns, who readily
patronize the shows and buy Mopp-rock or Brandy
Mopp-curls.

Cherry fairs were held in the cherry season on the
three Sundays in June, in the orchards between Fell Mill
and Shipston, and a fair of similar character was at one
time held in front of the " Three Stars " in Stratford.

Markets require but a moment's note. Many have
passed away, some as from inanition, others from various
causes. Chipping Kineton boasts its market-place, but the
thing itself has gone. Wellesbourne once had a market;
alas, it is no more.

In the good old days the cattle were sold in the open
street, and often one may see the stout rings, to which
they were tied, driven into the face of some convenient wall.
Rother Street marks the site of the old cattle market of
Stratford, and rings were *in situ* there until recently.

There is a story current that the farmers returning
from these markets were frequently robbed by a woman,
who hailed from Wimpston, and held ,the market-peart
husbandmen up after the most approved style of Dick
Turpin, and yet was never caught. On one or two occasions
it was a near squeak, since she had but time to escape
home and get into bed before she was called on by the
enraged man, whom she had robbed, and his friends.
The story runs, if they had only pulled down the bed-
clothes they would have seen her in her top boots.

The grant of a market involved some limit to its site.
In most places it ran through the chief street of its town.

Sometime in the reign of Henry III., fairly early,
Walter, son of William de Beauchamp, Lord of Alcester,

granted to his free burgesses and tenants, dwelling between the house of one Richard le Rous and Gunnild's bridge, the site of a market, to be held on Tuesday as custom enjoined. In this market the merchants and vendors of all kinds of flesh of animals, food corn, fine white wheat, barley, oats, peas, sold as they do in a modern market, side by side with merchants of drapery, linen, woollen goods, iron goods, honey, unguents, all kinds of fish, shoes, leather, leather goods, skins, wool, flax, geese, fowls, cheese, butter, eggs, salt, spices, " and all things known and unknown "—the last sufficiently comprehensive for even a London store of to-day. For this privilege a yearly rent of a halfpenny, payable at Michaelmas and the feast of St. Mary in March, was exacted. Great local magnates witnessed this deed, among them Sir Thomas de Camville, Sir Henry Hubant and Hugh Aguilon.

One can call up the picture of the merchants with their train of pack animals coming in over the narrow bridge from Warwick, Stratford, Droitwich and Worcester, and some from the queer town of Birmingham, a place that even much later had no walls or charter, so could not be punished by King Charles, as Coventry was.

Once started, markets were held and men gathered to buy and sell in peace and security under the " King's Peace."

The average man who attends a modern market probably concerns himself very little with its foundation. He only knows it is there, and useful to sell his cattle and corn and meet his fellow men; how it is that he is able to do so matters little. If any one of our readers is curious enough, he may wish to see a translation of the document that sturdy fighter Richard Cœur-de-Lion gave to the town of Stratford. It runs—

Richard, by the Grace of God, King of England, Duke of the Normans, Count of Aquitaine and Anjou, to the Archbishops, Bishops, Abbots, Earls, Barons, Justiciars, Shire-reeves, Reeves, Bailiffs, and all his ministers and faithful subjects, greeting. Be it known that We have granted, and by this our

present charter have confirmed, to our beloved in Christ, John,
Bishop of Worcester, and his successors, a market, to be held
for ever on Thursday in each week in his manor of Stratford.
Wherefore we will and firmly decree that the said Bishop and
his successors have the aforesaid market in perpetuity in his
manor of Stratford, every week on Thursday as is abovesaid,
well and in peace, freely and quietly, wholly and honorably, that
they may not be hindered or in any way molested.

The witnesses are Hubert, Archbishop of Canterbury,
Hugh, Bishop of Coventry, William of the church of
St. Mary, William son of Ralph the seneschal of Normandy, William de Hume, Constable of Normandy,
Robert de Court, and others whose names are not
recorded. The charter can be found in the *Liber Albus*
of the See, a valuable MS. rediscovered by the writer
after being lost sight of for more than a century.

That marketing was not all honey in the Middle
Ages appears from the following record in the Patent
Roll of 1400, ordering an inquiry—

wherefore certain lieges of the King, merchants and others,
were hindered from going by roads and highways between the
towns of Bermyngham and Stratford and the town of Alcestre,
to the markets of Coleshull, Bermyngham, Walshale and Dud-
leye, in the counties of Worcester and Warwick, and from
buying and selling therein. These said malefactors assembling
in conventicles, with their faces masked and dressed as torturers,
armed with machines called "gladmores," etc., lay in ambush,
assaulted the merchants, put them to flight, so that women and
children riding on horses, with their sacks filled with corn, not
only fell off, but some died, others were injured, and the sacks
were cut open and the corn scattered.

The above lends point to the old story recorded by
Dugdale of Alcock's arbour, a story still told among the
old folk of Haselor much as Dugdale told it. Alcock's
arbour is one of the two curiously isolated hills between
Stratford and Alcester which looks as if it were artificial,
but is not.

Towards the foot whereof is a hole, now almost filled up,
having been the entrance into a cave, as the inhabitants report,

of which cave there is an old wives story, that one Alcock, a great robber, used to lodge therein, and having got much money by that course of life, hid it in an iron-bound chest, whereunto there were three keys, which chest they say is still there, but guarded by a cock that continually sits upon it; and that on a time an Oxford scholar came thither, with a key that opened two of the locks, but as he was attempting to open the third, the cock seized him. To all which they adde, that of a bone of the partie, who set the cock there, could be brought, he would yield up the chest. (Dugdale, *Ant. of Warw.*, ed. Thomas, ii., p. 841.)

CHAPTER XVI.

Fast and Festival.

The year was marked in our forefathers' time by somewhat rare days when the whole village made holiday. It is true the rejoicings were more hearty than refined, but they were honest and real, looked eagerly forward to, and talked of when long past. The great feasts of the church's year combined revelry with religion, and dated back to the Sun festivals of most remote antiquity. Foremost of all came Yuletide or Christ's Mass.

The feast was held everywhere in honour of the completion of the Sun's yearly course. It held a place of conspicuous honour among the ancestors of our Saxon conquerors. Like all of our feasts, it began on the eve, when the Yule log was brought home.

There is little that is specially interesting preserved in the oral tradition of our Warwickshire folk, but in the conservative hamlets nestling in the foot-hills of the Cotswolds, ever the last preserve of old customs, men are living who have kept up the practice of mumming. The text of the Ilmington mummers is here given. The jokes and dialogue seem poor sort of stuff to retain such a hold through the centuries.*

The Mummers' patter as known in Ilmington.

Actors: The Caller, Molly, Jack, King George, Captain Thunderbolt, The Doctor, Beelzebub.

Caller.—In comes I, old mother Christmas,
   Welcome or welcome not.
   I hope old mother Christmas
   Will ne'er be forgot.

Molly.—Ladies and gentlemen all,
   My son has lately come home

---

* Br. i. 461. Brand's account is not very illuminating; the custom as known to the Cotswold villages is far more than a mere dressing up.

In a silver button waistcoat, three-legged hat. Calls the cat a bitch. As I went up, short, thin, straight, narrow. A crooked-looking lie. I saw a pig stye tied to an elder bush ; a house built of pancakes thatched with apple dumplings. I knocked at the maiden and out came the door, and asked if I could drink a crust full of ale and eat a glass of bread and cheese. I said no thank you, and meant if you please.

King George.—A room, a room, brave gallants all,
Pray give me room to ride,
I'm come to show activity
This merry Xmastide.
Activity of youth, activity of age,
I'll fight the first battle fought upon the stage.
Then where's the man that dares to stand,
I'll cut him down with my courageous hand.
I'll cut him, I'll hew him as small as flies
And send him to Satan to make mince pies.
Mince pies hot, mince pies cold,
I'll send him to Satan before he's three days old.

(Enter Captain Thunderbolt.)

Who be you ? What are you come for ?

Captain Thunderbolt.—I'm the man that dares to bid you stand.
You said you'd cut me down with thy courageous hand
And hew me small as flies,
And send me to Satan to make mince pies.
Mince pies hot, mince pies cold,
Thou said'st thou'd send me to Satan before I was three days old.
Mind thy head and guard the blow,
Mind your nose, your head also.

(They fight, King George falls.)

Molly.—Doctor ! doctor ! do thy part,
King George is wounded through the heart.
Through the heart and through the knee,
Ten guineas to thee I'll freely gie.

(Enter the Doctor.)

Come in Jack Viney.

Doctor.—My name is not Jack Viney, my name is
    Mr. Viney. A man of great fame. I can do
    more than you or any man can.

Molly.—Oh, what can you do?

Doctor.—I can cure a magpie of the toothache.

Molly.—How should you do that?

Doctor.—Lay his body on a stool and cut his head off.

Molly.—That would kill him, you fool.

Doctor.—Well then, I could lay his head upon a stool
    and cut his body off.

Molly.—What else can you do?

Doctor.—I can cure the itch, the stitch, the palsey, and
    gout,
    Pains within and pains without.
    Hump, hump, hump! the mulleygrubs and all other
    vainglorious diseases. I can cure this man if he's
    not quite dead.
    Bold fellow, raise up thy head.

                (*Molly cries and says King George wants a
                            tooth drawn.*)

Doctor.—Jack, fetch my instruments.

Jack.—I shan't.

Doctor.—What's that?

Jack.—I shan't. (*Doctor runs after him.*)
    This it, Sir?

Doctor.—No.

Jack.—Well, is this it?

Doctor.—No, you fool. (*Kicks him out.*)

    (*Jack brings in a pair of tongs and all four try to pull
    out the tooth, and all fall down, Molly showing
    her man's breeches. The Doctor gets up with the
    tongs and a tooth.*)

    Ladies and gentlemen all, how this poor old man
    must have suffered. Here's a tooth as long and as
    strong as a tenpenny nail. Oh, how he must have
    suffered!
    In my box I carry a pill,
    In my bottle I carry a smell,
    In my hand there is no disdain,
    Rise up, King George, and fight again.

I

Beelzebub.—In comes I, old Beelzebub,
    At my shoulder I carry a club,
    In my hand a dripping pan.
    Don't you think I'm a jolly old man?
Fiddler.—In come I which aint been it.
    My great yed and little wit.
    My yeds so big, my wits so small,
    I've brought my fiddle to please you all.
    Green sleeves and yellow waist
    Hop and jump about like pease.
    And I was a fiddling a battle of pea soup and lead,
      a shot come through my elbow and spoilt all my
      scraping.

                  (All dance.)

The mummers, dressed in their masquerade, went from house to house, and were entertained in the usual manner. What they desired to express beyond rough jollity does not appear.

The men of Wimpstone still go round carol singing, but only a few scraps of ancient carols have been handed down. Those now sung are taken from the printed collections; but see page 147.

The decoration of houses was almost confined to holly in old days; sprigs of this tree were fixed in the leaden frames of the quarries which filled the windows and showed from the outside. Larger boughs were placed wherever they could be fastened, as on the bacon rack or over the hearth. In the time of Stow not only holme but ivy and bay "and whatsoever is green" was used, and in 1765 laurel, box, rosemary. In rare instances yew and mistletoe are recorded. In spite of the now general use of the last, there is very little notice of it in legend, and indeed it seems to have been regarded more as a hurtful thing than a pleasant one, though it had in some parts many virtues attributed to it. Sir John Colbatch* says it is not only a cure for epilepsy, but drives away evil spirits. Brand alludes to its being hung in kitchens, where any female standing beneath it might expect to be kissed by the young men. The custom

* Br. i. 524.

must then have been a rare one.* It has certainly become popular since.

Nothing noteworthy has been heard from the old men concerning either New Year's Day or Twelfth Day, though on the latter wassailing was practised in the neighbouring counties, and the health of the apple trees in the orchard drank with due ceremony.

February 2nd, the feast of the Purification of the Blessed Mary the Virgin, was known to our forefathers as Candlemas Day, because on that day the churches were decorated with candles and they were borne in procession. Nothing of this is left to us in the country lore of Warwickshire, only a weather rhyme :—

> If Candlemas Day be fair and bright
> Winter will have another flight.
> If Candlemas Day be wind and rain
> Winter is gone and won't come again.

On this day all Christmas decorations should be taken down and burnt, otherwise ill luck will follow.†

The next feast that has left a mark on the people's traditions is that of St. Valentine, when according to early authority the birds began to mate. Humanity thought it a very pretty idea that they, half in jest, should choose " for their Valentine " some rustic beauty and send her a present on this day. In Armscot the boys of the village went round singing for apples, which were preserved and fried into fritters. As they went they sang—

> Good morrow Valentine,
> First its yours, then its mine,
> Please give I a Valentine.

On Shrove Tuesday the Ilmington ringers began the day with a peal on the church bells, then sounded the pancake bell, originally instituted to warn the faithful to come to be shriven, but afterwards became merely a professional notice by the parish clerk that he was about to make his yearly visitation of the farms to collect his per-

* Br. i. 524.   † Br. i. 49.

quisite of pancakes, which he and the five ringers did in
a large basket lined with flannel, singing—

> Link it, Lank it
> Gie me a pankit.

The provision of pancakes by the good housewife was
no sinecure. On one occasion the farmer's wife offered
her odd man a meal of them and he ate 22 ! on asking if
he wanted more, he said "he could do with another."
The good woman wept !

There is an old saying that "If I were in bed with
my hands full of pancakes I wouldn't get up to supper."

The pancake bell rang out at Tredington, where old
Stephen Rollandson, the clerk, went his round. The
bell was in the like manner sounded in many places, but
whether for the same purpose or not one does not know.
It is duly recorded from Bidford and Aston Cantlow, and
many other Warwickshire parishes, including Allesley,
Bedworth, Clifton, Coventry and Grandborough.

In the large towns Curfew was rung at 8 p.m., as at
Brailes, Knowle, Nuneaton, Rugby and Stratford-on-Avon.
At Brailes a bell sounded at 6 a.m., while at Honington a
Mass bell sounded at 9 a.m. The bell that ushered in
the gleaning rang at Ettington and at Cubbington. The
Pudding bell rang at Kineton after morning service on
Sundays to show that it was time to put the puddings in
for the midday dinner.

The middle Sunday in Lent, Mothering Sunday, was
generally kept as the day apprentices came home to visit
their parents, and were regaled with special fare. At
Shipston on Stour the chief dish was Furmatty, prepared
as follows : The wheat was placed, a small quantity at a
time, in a bag, which was then laid upon the floor and
beaten with a stick to separate the husk from the grain,
after which it was boiled with plums to make a sort of
pudding.

Palm Sunday, in early documents *Dominica in ramis
Palmarum*, is only recognised locally as the day to gather
"palms," i.e., the male catkins of the Goat Willow,

in memory of Our Lord's entry into Jerusalem. These were formerly blessed in church by the priest vested in a red cope. At Kempton in Herefordshire it was customary to eat figs on this day,* but inquiry failed to discover any such tradition in Warwickshire.

Good Friday is still the usual day for the labourers to plant potatoes, advantage being taken of the holiday, and after church the men set to work, but as pointed out above no woman would wash clothes on this day. Hot Cross buns are known to everyone and are still in general request ; the cross with which they were marked is common both to them and other kinds of cakes and bread, and originated in the early Christian practice of making the Holy Sign on all objects used, to eject the Devil and his minions. Saffron is used in some of the local bakehouses for these buns.

Easter Day was heralded in in ancient days by a uniquely interesting custom. The young men of Coleshill went out into the fields early in the morning to catch or endeavour to catch a hare ; if they were successful the captors in a body took their capture to the rectory, and the rector by immemorial usage was bound to provide them with a breakfast of a calf's head and a hundred eggs. A similar custom was known at Wootton Wawen.

The Birmingham Church Clipping on Easter Day is recorded by Hone† in these words :—

When I was a child as sure as Easter Monday came I was taken to see the children clip the churches. This ceremony was performed amid crowds of people and shouts of joy by the children of the different charity schools, who at a certain hour flocked together for that purpose. The first comers placed themselves hand in hand with their backs against the church and were joined by their companions, who gradually increased in number till the chain was at last of sufficient length completely to surround the sacred edifice. As soon as the hand of the last of the train had grasped that of the first the party broke up and walked in procession to the other church, where the ceremony was repeated.

* Br. i. 124.
† *Every Day Book*, i. 431.

Easter Monday and Tuesday were known as Heaving Day,* because on the former day in Warwickshire it was customary for the men to heave and kiss the women, and on the Tuesday the women did the like to the men. The women's heaving day was the most amusing. " Many a time I have passed along the streets inhabited by the lower orders of the people and seen parties of jolly matrons assembled round tables, on which stood a foaming tankard of ale. There they sate, in pride of absolute sovereignty, and woe betide the luckless man that dare invade their prerogatives ; as sure as he was seen he was pursued, and as sure as he was pursued he was taken, and as sure as he was taken he was heaved and kissed, and compelled to pay sixpence for ' leave and licence ' to depart." Also Brand cites an extract showing the custom to have taken place in the 18th year of Edward I., 1289, when the King himself was "lifted " by the ladies of the bedchamber. This curious ceremony is supposed to be in honour of the Resurrection of Our Lord.

The second Tuesday after Easter is one of the days of Hoke Tide, when the men *hoc* the women on Monday and the women the men on Tuesday. On both days both sexes intercepted the passage of the British public along the King's way by stretching ropes across and demanding a fee for some supposedly pious use.

It would seem that Hoke Day was held, properly speaking, on that day known as Quindena Paschæ, but as this would be the second Sunday after Easter this must have been transferred to the Monday and Tuesday following ; Matthew Paris says Tuesday. In any case Leicester provided a repetition of the ceremony among his other entertainments at his Castle of Kenilworth for the amusement of Elizabeth.

And that there might be nothing wanting that these parts could afford, hither came the Coventre men, and acted the ancient play, long since used in that city, called Hocke-Tuesday, setting forth the destruction of the Danes in King Ethelred's

* Br. i. 183.

time, with which the Queen was so pleased that she gave them a brace of bucks and five marks in money to bear the charges of a feast. (Dugdale, *Ant. of Warwickshire*, 1656 ed., p. 166.)

According to Laneham the play set forth how the Danes were for quietness borne and allowed to remain in peace withal, until, on the said St. Brice's night, they were all despatched and the realm rid ; and because the matter did show in actions and rhymes how valiantly our English women for the love of their country behaved, the men of Coventry thought it might move some mirth in Her Majesty. The thing they said is grounded in story, and for pastime was wont to be played in our city yearly, without ill example of manners, papistry or any other superstition, and they knew no cause why it was late laid down, "unless it was by the zeal of certain of their preachers, men very commendable for their behaviour and learning, and sweet in their sermons, but somewhat too sour in preaching away their pastime." By licence therefore they got up their Hock-tide play at Kenilworth, wherein Capt. Cox . . . . came marching on valiantly before, clean trussed and garnished above the knee, all fresh in a velvet cap, with his ton-sword, and another fence-master with him, making room for the rest. Then came proudly the Danish knights on horseback and then the English, each with his alder-pole martially in his hand. The meeting at first waxing warm, then kindled with courage on both sides into a hot skirmish, and from that into a blazing battle with spear and shield, so that by outrageous races and fierce encounters horse and man sometimes tumbled into the dust. Then they fell to with sword and target, and did clang and bang till the fight so ceasing ; afterwards followed the foot of both hosts, one after the other marching, wheeling, forming into squadrons, triangles, and circles, and so out again ; then got they so grisly together that, inflamed on both sides, twice the Danes had the better, but at last were quelled, and so being wholly vanquished many were led in triumph by our English women. This manner of good pastime was fought under the window of her highness . . . .*

It should be remembered that Easter Day required that something new should be worn to prevent ill-luck. The superstition, if such it deserves to be called, is widespread.

The very ancient guild of the Holy Cross of Strat-ford-upon-Avon held its feast at an early date in Easter week. The rules stated that the feast must be "in such a manner that brotherly love shall be cherished among them and evil-speaking driven out, that peace shall always dwell among them and true love be upheld, and every sister of the guild shall bring with her to the feast a great tankard, and all the tankards shall be filled with ale, and afterwards the ale shall be given to the poor—so likewise shall the brethren do . . . . and before any brother or sister shall touch the feast in the hall, all those gathered shall put up their prayers, that God, the blessed Virgin Mary, and the Much-to-be-venerated Cross, in whose honour they have come together, will keep them from all harm and ill." It is rather a pity that guilds holding such sentiments have ceased to exist; there might be a little less malice, hatred and envy in this speed-mad world of to-day if they were still with us.

It is perhaps worth while to give an account from the Compotus rolls of the same guild to show what sort of provision was made for the annual rejoicing. In 1467 8 quarters of corn at 5s. the quarter; 12 quarters of malt at 3s. 6d. a quarter was provided for ale-brewing; for baking bread 16½d.; for strayner clothes 4d.; Alice Barber received for her work in brewing 2 quarts of ale and 16d.; coal and fuel cost 2s.; 13 calves at 13d. each; 26 lambs at 12d. each; beef, marybones, veal, etc.; 1 kid at 16d.; half a pound of cinnamon 2s.; half a pound of ginger 12d.; half a pound of saunders 20d.; agnis seede 1d.; three gallons of honey 4s.; white sugar 14d.; milk at 1d. a gallon; creme at 8d. a gallon; 120 pullets at 10s.; 950 eggs at 6s. a hundred; 3 small pigs

* Br. i. 189.

at 18*d.*, etc. Verily there was plenty of good cheer on this occasion.

At a later date the annual banquet was removed to Ascension-tide, which it is now necessary to consider.

The three days before Ascension Day were called Rogation days, and on these days the clergy, church-wardens and other principal inhabitants perambulated the parish boundary, where at the stated points the boys of the village were suitably impressed with the actual position of the boundary in question by being bumped, beaten or dipped, or some other equally rough treatment, to impress the spot upon their memory in an indelible fashion. Brand quotes from Hone's *Year Book* : That on enquiry if some point was a boundary, a man replied, " 'Ees, that it is, I'm sure o't by the same token that I were toss'd into't, and paddled about there like a water-rot till I wor half dead." On these occasions much ale and a minimum of bread was consumed at the expense of the parish. The custom is locally either extinct or nearly so.

May Day, the feast of the Saints Philip and James, is hardly a church festival; so far as its customs are con-cerned, the festival seems to be an entirely pagan one. It was very generally observed both in London and the country.

In Stratford-upon-Avon branches of green trees are carried about to-day as in the past, adorned by ribbons and rags of bright colours, the object being to extract divers coppers from the passers by, but these garlands are very primitive. It is rare to obtain any " May " in flower for them by the 1st of the month, and, on the other hand, it is accounted most unlucky to bring a bough of that shrub indoors before this date.

May Day was held in full honour on the Alscot estate and in accordance with traditional custom, a very different thing from a modern revival of something that has dropped into disuse, which is not at all the same thing and never very successful. The children of the four villages forming the estate collected flowers on the

even, which were made into garlands consisting of a
double hoop attached to a long pole. Each of the
parishes had a garland, and they were taken to the hall in
the morning, and the squire and his wife and family
heard the May songs sung, and regaled the young folk
with cakes and cowslip wine. Then they all returned
and made a long perambulation of the farms, bearing
their May garland with them. A tea was provided in
part from the sums the children obtained on the journey-
ings. Games in the Park closed the day.

The only permanent May-pole left in the neighbourhood stands at the west end of the village of Welford-on-
Avon. It is not as tall as the older pole, which blew
down in a gale. The pole is one of the places of meeting
for the South Warwickshire hounds. It stands surrounded by a circular quickset hedge upon a mound,
and is painted in red and white spirals to the summit,
which is surmounted by a weather vane.

It is on record that the young men of Ebrington
made up their minds that they would have the finest May-
pole in the whole country side. Some twenty of them
accordingly went to the woods of Burnt Norton and cut
down a larch tree some 40 feet in length, carried it home
with them, dug the hole, and raised it bedecked with
garlands. In the morning the good people of the place
saw to their surprise the lofty pole, and it proved such
an attraction that ere the day was over the inhabitants of
places as far distant as Evesham came to see the wonder.
The story shows that our ancestors spared neither toil
nor trouble to gain their ends when urged by custom.

The day was observed at Shipston-on-Stour, Tredington and Stratford-upon-Avon by the sweeps with their
own garland. Those who took part did so in fantastic
attire, reminding one of the Jack-in-the-green and his
attendants described by Brand.[*]

Charles I. specially mentions May-poles in his warrant
of Oct. 18th, 1633, but they were ordered to be destroyed
by the Puritan ordinance of 1644 because of the pro-

* Br. i. 231.

fanation of the Lord's Day. They are herein called "a heathenish vanity, generally abused by superstition and wickedness." After the Restoration they were very wisely allowed again, and the young men and maidens danced about them and chose their May Queen as before.

Whitsunday seems to have been one of the special days celebrated with Morris-dancing, but this dance was also in request on May Day, and at Bideford is still used on Trinity Monday. The Morris dancers of Ilmington and Bidford have never dropped their ancient skill, and have a great reputation at the present time, having danced before the King on at least one occasion by royal command.

The dance is performed by ten men, who are dressed in breeches and white shirts. The fiddler, who now takes the place of the old piper, with his pipe and tabor, alone wears a hat; the others, except "Maid Marion," are bareheaded. They wear sashes over their shirts and bells fastened to straps buckled round their knees. Maid Marion wears an embroidered petticoat. Laneham speaks of "six dauncers, Mawd Marion, and a fool." So that the number has increased since his day.

Maid Marion was originally the Queen of the May and mistress of the Archery games, and as such associated with Robin Hood. How she became the fool is not easy to say. The idea of the Queen needing a king in the May festivity probably brought in Robin Hood as a suitable royal spouse for the May Queen. The dancers in the old tradition carried napkins, as they still do, or short wooden staves. Mr. Samuel Bennet of Ilmington, whose knowledge of the old lore of his parish is very great, showed the writer the old tabor formerly in use.

At Whitsuntide in Wootton Wawen as late as 1768 it was the custom for the women of the village to go round to the farms milking the cows. This milk they kept, dividing it between them, and from it made Frumentary, which in this place consisted of the milk, wheat, sugar and spice.

Oak Apple Day, May the 29th, commemorates the

day on which the fugitive Charles II. hid in an oak tree on his escape from his enemies after the battle of Worcester. It is still the custom to wear an oak-apple on this day. The boys of Long Marston grammar school did this, and, moreover, punished any boy who might have neglected this sign of loyalty by stinging him with nettles ; the sprig of oak was often hidden until the critical moment arrived, and produced to the discomfiture of his would-have-been tormentor.

Coventry Show Fair cannot be passed over without a brief mention. It began on the Friday in Trinity week and lasted eight days. Its great feature was the Lady Godiva procession and Peeping Tom.

The story has been printed and reprinted in many a ballad and broadside. Earl Leofric, grievously offended with the good folk of Coventry, laid heavy taxes upon them. The people appealed to Lady Godiva, the Earl's wife, to intercede for them. She succeeded in obtaining from the Earl a promise that he would repeal the taxes if she would ride naked through the streets of the city, meaning that no persuasion whatever should prevail with him ; she, good and pious soul, deeply touched by the distress of the citizens, accepted the harsh terms. She sent an order to the city rulers that all doors and windows should be shut and no one look out on pain of death. Then she rode through the city covered only by her beautiful hair. None saw her but a poor taylor, who looked out of his upper window, where his figure watches to-day. He was visited with blindness for his sin. In the windows of Trinity church were at one time the effigies of the Earl and Countess with this couplet—

I, Luriche, for love of thee
Do set Coventry toll free.

The show was not apparently established until the reign of Charles II., so that the Godiva episode is not a remnant of medieval lore.

St. Barnabas Day, June 11th, is still remembered at Ilmington by the rhyme—

> Barnaby bright, Barnaby bright,
> Longest day, shortest night.

Corpus Christi Day is mentioned by Dugdale* as the day on which the famous mystery play, preserved in the British Museum,† was acted in that city. The play was edited from this MS. in 1841 for the Shakespeare Society. No local tradition seems to be preserved.

St. Vitus, commemorated on June 15th, has given his name to a disease called locally the Viper's Dance. An old inhabitant of Wimpston, speaking of a somewhat peculiar lady of the neighbourhood, said of her, "she allus were funny ever since she had the Viper's dance."

Midsummer Eve and Day, which figure so largely in the folk lore of many counties, seem to have left no trace in the recollection of the people of South Warwickshire, though in Oxfordshire there is some remembrance of Midsummer fires.

St. Swithin's Day, July 15th, is known here as elsewhere by the general saying that if it rains on St. Swithin's Day it will be wet for forty days. The story is supposed to be derived from the annoyance of the Saint at the removal of his remains, but is a comparatively late invention, which has somehow "caught on."

The Gule of August, Lammas Day, was the appointed day on which the flocks of the community were depastured on the Lammas pastures. It is, of course, the Feast of St. Peter in Chains.

The Feast of the Nativity of the Blessed Mary the Virgin may serve to remind us of the many native plants that bear her name, notably Lady's Bedstraw (*Galium verum*), Lady's Mantle (*Alchemilla*), Lady's Slipper, called also Venus's Slipper (*Cypripedium*), Lady's Smock (*Cardamine pratensis*), and Lady's Tresses (*Spiranthes*).

From Mr. F. S. Potter the writer heard the legend

---

* *Ant. of Warwickshire.*   † Cott. MS. Vesp. D. vii.

that September 21st is the Devil's Nutting-day. There is a vague story to account for the name, "The Devil's bag of nuts," by which name a curious conical hill on the road between Alcester and Stratford is known. Here the Devil had taken his fill of nuts, and was making off with them, but at the intercession of Our Lady was forced to fling them down in haste, and they turned into this hill. The usual traditional nutting day was fixed upon the Feast of the Exaltation of the Holy Cross, September the 14th.* Brand quotes from Poor Robin 1709 :—

> The Devil as common people say
> Doth go a nutting on Holy-rood day.

Many superstitions gathered in most places about Allhallowe'en, All Saints Day itself and All Souls ; in most counties love charms were in great request by the maidens of the villages, but there is little record of such practices in the district we are dealing with, nothing in fact worthy of notice.

It should, however, be remembered how great a part the Saints played in England in days of old. Documents are almost invariably dated by their feasts, the formula being the eve, morrow, or Monday, Tuesday or some day next after the Feast of the Saint. As such days were holidays, no doubt witnesses could be easier found, and in fact the actual feast day itself is the more often chosen for the transaction. The names of little-known local Saints are useful as a means of tracing the religious house or diocese in which an early liturgical manuscript was written, a matter of some little importance.

In Sir William Dugdale's *Diary* he says, "On All-Hallow e'en the master of the family anciently used to carry a bunch of straw, fired about his corn, saying—

> Fire and Red low
> Light on my teen Low."

As Dugdale was a Warwickshire man it is likely the

---

* Br. i. 353.

custom was in use in his neighbourhood. Brand mentions other instances of "Tindles."*

He quotes also that in Warwickshire his servant told him that it was customary to have seed cake at All-Hallows, and at the end of wheat seed time, and at the end of barley and bean seed time, to give the ploughmen froise, which is a kind of thick pancake.

November the fifth is one of the days still popular among us. Grotesque figures are even now borne round, while bonfires and fireworks are in general use. Material for the fire was collected at Long Marston to the recitation of the following :—

> Please to remember the fifth of November.
> Gunpowder plot
> Shall never be forgot
> As long as old England is tied in a knot.
> A stick and a stake
> For King George's sake.
> Will you please give us a faggot.
> If you wont give one we'll steal two,
> The better for we and the worse for you.

St. Thomas's Day, December the 21st, is the day fixed by common custom for the widows and other old women of the parish to go gooding or Thomasing. A systematic visitation of the farms took place and the money collected was divided; as a matter of course refreshment was offered, and some of the women reached home with difficulty or even not at all. At Tredington only the children went, and at Halford the children had a half-holiday for the purpose.

The church bell was rung in many places to mark the day. This practice prevailed at Wellesbourne, Kineton, Fenny Compton, but at Wellesbourne the day was changed by the Vicar to that of the patron saint, St. Peter, in ignorance one may suppose of its meaning.

Speaking of bells at Ilmington, the "Devil's peal" was rung on New Year's Day, and in the same place, when a ringer died, his body was chimed to church.

* Br. i. 391

CHAPTER XVII.

FOLK RHYMES.

The rustics of South Warwickshire in the days of old were exceedingly fond of jingling rhyme, and used it, not only on their tombstones, but on all sorts of occasions, whenever anything at all out of the common happened. Indeed it was not entirely unknown as a form of advertisement. The Birch family, tinkers of Ilmington, wandered into most of the villages round with this doggerel on their cart :—

> George Birch the tinker is my name
> And from Ilmington I came,
> Scissors and razors bring this way
> And I will grind them well to-day.

Another member of the family, Abraham Birch, came round attired in a waistcoat with shillings in lieu of buttons and half-crowns sewn on his coat. His version is not at all original. It ran :—

> Abraham Birch is my name,
> England is my nation,
> Ilmington my dwelling place,
> And Christ is my salvation.

Henry varied his placard as follows :—

> Henry Birch is my name,
> And from Ilmington I came,
> Tin man and brazier is my trade,
> To work for pay I here have strayed.
> Your pots and kettles bring this way,
> And I will mend them well to-day.

These people were honest and good artificers and very much sought after in their day. Their successors are not to be found.

The modern Romeo does not usually approach his prospective father-in-law in verse, but an Ilmington

bricklayer sent Abraham the following, which is certainly
very much to the point and avoids saying too much :—

> A few more bricks, a little more mortar,
> Please Mr. Birch let me have your daughter.

As he deserved, he won the charming Miss Birch, but
whether they lived happily ever after legend sayeth not.

Rhyme came in useful as a warning on at least one
occasion. This scroll was found fixed on the fence of the
new enclosure of the common fields of Winderton :—

> There's hedges and ditches quick to be found,
> Postis and rails cut out and put down,
> And when you have finished and hung up your gates,
> Some of you'll be glad to sell your estates.

Of far greater ambition are some of the efforts of the
man who styled himself " the poet Handy." There are
in existence in print long ballads of his composing, which
presumably had a local sale. The following gem speaks
of his genius. It was found affixed to his cottage gate
after a few words with his " missus."

> Of all the donkeys on the green,
> And all the pigs within the sty,
> There's none as unkid as my old girl,
> When she's a mind to try.

It is almost equalled by the notice hung up after the
repair of the author's well :—

> Old Sammy Harris drew these stones,
> The poet Handy built them in.
> Here you may come and drink your fill
> Of water, *pure as gin.*

The old inhabitants of Ilmington had an hereditary
love of poking fun at their Gloucestershire neighbours,
over the hill top in Ebrington, whom they styled
"mawms," another name for fools. The series has never
appeared in print so far as the writer is aware, but is
important in the study of folk rhyme.

The first is said to perpetuate a practical joke played
by a party of young men with the unwilling aid of a

K

donkey. It seems a difficult feat, but one has to remember how low the old English cottage was—

> Mrs. Morris got up to brew,
> There was sumot the matter with the chimbley flue.
> Master Morris got up to see
> A donkey's legs down his chimbeley.
> The donkey was stuck in the chimbly top,
> And his tail behind went flipperty flop.
> The donkey belonged to Benjamin Harris,
> And they took him to Moreton to swear his parish.

The Yebberton mawms were so silly that they were supposed to try and raise the church tower higher by mucking it. Hence—

> Master Southam, a man of gret power,
> Lent a horse and cart to muck the church tower.
> They mucked the tower to make it grow high,
> But not as lofty as the sky,
> And when the muck began to sink
> They swore the tower had grown an inch.
> Rummy dum darey, Flare up Mary,
> Whoever did hear of such wonderful times.

Rejoicing for the victory of Waterloo nearly cost the people of Ebrington their church, and led the Ilmington folk to compose the following :—

> The Yebberton mawms to show their power
> They lit a fire atop of the tower.
> The lead ran down like blood from a slaughter,
> The old women ran to catch the soft water.
> There was a blind man who wanted to see,
> They bunted him up in a gooseberry.
> He swore it was his hearty desire
> To see the top of the tower afire.

Another of these rhymes is of greater interest, since it seems very similar to the West of England tales of the Moonrakers. As a matter of fact it refers to the local charity cows, already mentioned—

> One moonlight night when it did freeze,
> The moon shone in the pool, they thought it was a cheese.
> They fetch'd some rakes to rake about,
> Then swore they couldn't get it out.

Some of the recipients of the charity milk pooled their milk and made a cheese from it, and having indulged rather too freely on the way home let it fall into the pool, and were in no state to get it out again. Still, the coincidence with the Western legend is curious.

Yet another rhyme alludes to the ancient idea that a certain cure for hydrophobia lay in a dip in the sea—

> The Yebberton mawms to Campden went,
> To buy a wheel barrow was their intent.
> They carried the barrow from Campden town,
> For fear that its wheels should bruise the ground.
> There was a mad dog come through the town,
> And bit the side of the barrow all round.
> They took it to the sea to be dipped,
> And swore the dog he should be whipt.

Bad as these rhymes are, there is worse to come. At Wimpstone the local efforts never rose above a string of names, such as—

> Johnny Hiatt of Mousetrap Hall,
> Ward's among the rushes,
> Thomas Miles of Radbrooke Hall,
> And Ashby at the bushes.

All of them local farmers.

Village rivalry is no new thing, it always was and always will be. Witness this quatrain :—

> The Armscot boys are very good boys,
> The Nobold* boys are better,
> The Halford boys can stand on one leg,
> And kick them all into the gutter.

One more specimen, this time the outcome of an Alderminster blacksmith named Hutchins :—

> The plough is done and finished quite,
> I'm going to bring it home tonight.
> You promised me right straight and fair
> You'd let me have a quart of beer.

The models on which these scraps of jingle were produced must surely have been derived from the ballad

* Newbold on Stour.

literature sold by travelling hawkers at fairs and wakes. It is interesting to see that the uneducated mind clung somehow throughout the ages to some faint taste for poetry, if one can dignify such verses by such a name.

This is perhaps a good place to allude to a class of sayings of obscure origin, taking the form of homely proverbs. The following are examples :—

"He's like Hunt's dog, he'll neither go to church nor stay at home." Who Hunt was is difficult to say. That the saying gibes at a man who cannot make up his mind seems plain.

"He's like old Berry's wife, just the thing." Here again no one knows whether there ever was such a person as old Berry. His wife, as wives go, seems to be highly praised.

"He's like Busson's father, always behind." The author of this gem did not believe in the adage "better late than never."

"Cox's pig thought a lie, he thought he was going to have his breakfast when 'twas the butcher come to kill him." A timely warning against too great optimism.

That the ancient ballad itself is not entirely forgotten is an astonishing fact, though Mr. Scarlett Potter said that in his young days hardly a fragment was left of the early songs of the county. He could only collect a few unimportant fragments. Yet the writer has himself heard an old lady, well over ninety, sing to him the long and well-known early ballad of "The Cruel Gardener," which begins—

> Come all young lovers, to me lend an ear,
> Take heed to this sad story given here.
> 'Tis of a maiden fair,
> A shepherdess we hear,
> And little Cupid did her heart ensnare.

One of the verses enshrines a fragment of folk lore,

and for that reason should be preserved here, though
quoted in Brand, iii. 217—

> Mother! said he, most cruel and severe,
> I'm afraid you've killed my joy and only dear,
> For a dove I doe declare
> Did all in blood appear.
> But if that she is dead, her fate I'll share.

The same old lady repeated the ballad of the Lord
Thomas—

> Lord Thomas was a forester
> And a chaser of the King's deer,
> Fair Ellenor was a fair young woman,
> Lord Thomas he loved her dear.
> Come riddle my riddle, dear mother, he said,
> And riddle us both in one,
> Whether I shall marry with fair Ellenor
> And leave the brown girl alone.
>
> The brown girl she has houses and lands,
> Fair Ellenor she has none ;
> Therefore I charge thee on my blessing
> To bring the brown girl home.
> Lord Thomas he went to fair Ellenor's bower,
> And knocked at the ring,
> And none was so ready as fair Ellenor
> To let Sir Thomas in.

and so for twenty-five verses or more to the tragedy at
the end.

CHAPTER XVIII.

THE POOR.

In the days of our Saxon forefathers every peasant who was homeless was required to reside with some householder under pain of losing his status as a member of the community. He lost his folk-right unless he could find the protection of some lord in the folkmote. The householder was held to be responsible for all the inmates of his house, whether bond or free, once he granted him admission beneath his roof, even if the person in question was but a temporary visitor.

The age-long struggle between riches and poverty thus began. Industry on the one hand, idleness on the other, were dealt with by the opinion of their fellows, an opinion which resulted in much that we should now consider cruel and vindictive. The rude customs of the half civilized were not very prone to sentimental pity ; perhaps we of to-day may have gone a little too far in the other respect. Officially the poor for several centuries were looked upon as criminals, the aged and infirm as encumbrances; if they had not eked out a miserable existence by begging they would inevitably have starved. In the thirteenth century robbery by violence was rife— witness the provisions of the Statute of Winchester 1285, which, after reciting proof of the evil state of the country-side, enact that the Hundred is to be responsible for all robberies within its bounds ; the gates of towns must be closed from sunset to sunrise. The King's way is to be cleared of such undergrowth as might serve to hide a felon, and widened, that men might go about their business in peace, and no cover serve to conceal a robber. The breakdown of feudalism, which began *temp.* Edw. II., led to wages being paid rather than service rendered, but it certainly served to increase vagrancy, only too often combined violence. The act of 13 Edward II., cap. 14

(1332), endeavoured to suppress such lawless poverty, and in particular the bands of roberdes-men, wastors and draw-latches, who were to be arrested and imprisoned. To be a beggar was to be a vagrant—the law made no distinction ; it suppressed both, or did its best to do so. No one suggested that any means of livelihood should be found for these outcasts.

In 1349 the Statute of Labourers was enacted. It ordered all men to give their services to such as needed them, without an increase in their former rate of pay as sanctioned by ancient custom, under pain of imprisonment for refusal. This provision was foredoomed to failure, since the Black Death made the supply of available labour altogether inadequate. The wages ordered were Haymaking 1d. a day, Mowing 5d. an acre, Reaping 2d. or 3d. a day, and so forth, the value of the penny being very much larger than now—how much larger is difficult to say. It was unfortunate for the legislators that the law was introduced at a time it could not succeed, since it neither benefited the husbandman nor his dependents. Men left their manor or village and hired themselves, naturally enough, where they could get the best pay.

In 1360 it was ordered that persons absenting themselves from their proper work should be branded on the forehead with the letter F ; even this barbarous order made but little difference.

All the efforts of the law, however strongly worded, to enforce a national rate of wages failed to meet the serious disorders which grew and increased under Rich. II., and were especially bad in the Marches of Wales. The efforts of the feudal lords to retain their rights over their vassals only fanned the revolt ; the old system was out of touch with the times and could not be renewed. In the meantime class hatred grew to an unprecedented extent.

An attempt was made in 1388 by means of a Poor Law statute. It laid down that servants and labourers were prohibited from wandering, a regular payment was fixed, and towns were to support beggars who could not work ; these were forced to withdraw to the place in which they were born and there abide for life, but no fixed provision was made for their support, they had to exist on chance alms. Needless to say this regulation did not meet with greater success than its predecessors.

The state of the submerged improved in the early days of the fifteenth century, since general conditions became far better owing to a rise in prosperity and general outlook, and increased trade. Love of freedom, in part due to the break-up of vassalage, led to a revival, the increase of town populations, and wider mental outlook. There was nevertheless something lost, viz., the protection of the lord, since so long as a dependent served his lord in the humblest capacity he was not in want of a home, or the means and tools to gain a frugal and rough livelihood. This applied only to those who held by servile tenure ; the freeholders who failed, parted with their lands as they could no longer perform the required services, and fell in status and wandered far afield from the place that knew them, becoming legally poor. Relief of some sort thus became a pressing need.

There had always been religious houses and hospitals wherein all were fed and had a night's lodging, with no question asked. In the hospitals lepers, the insane, and women with child were supposed to be provided for, but the funds of many were so reduced by the visitations of the various waves of the Black Death, and by abuse, neglect and misappropriation, that Henry V. issued an inquiry into their management.

The weak and half crazy Henry VI. indirectly caused vast misery, due in part to the rivalry of the great Houses of York and Lancaster, so that retrograde enactments were forced on an unwilling nation. New tables of prices were issued, but no minimum was fixed ; men were so driven by poverty that they were compelled to accept lower wages than the statute ordained. Unrest and discontent were rife.

Under Henry VII. imprisonment for this cause was softened down to sitting in the stocks with a sparing supply of bread and water. Once again beggars who could not gain employment were ordered to return to their hundred, or to the place they were best known, or their birthplace. This scarcity of jobs to go round was largely due to the depopulation of the villages, in many of which large stretches of arable land had been laid down for pasture ; but the sick, and women with child, were for the first time treated more tenderly, yet labourers were expected to work fourteen hours daily with intervals of half-an-hour for breakfast and one and a-half for dinner and rest.

By the act of 22 Henry VIII., cap. 12 (1530-31), the registration of beggars by the Custos Rotulorum was authorized ; a letter was given to the recipient allowing him to beg within specified limits. Those who did so without this licence were whipped and set in the stocks ; sturdy beggars were ordered to be whipped at the cart-tail through the next market town until their bodies were bloody. Then they were put upon their oath to return to their birthplaces and put themselves to labour " as a true man should do." This was altered somewhat by the act of 27 Henry VIII., cap. 25 (1535-6), by which valiant beggars were to be set to work and kept to continual labour to get their own living ; the poor incapable of doing so were to be relieved, at the cost of their parish, by the constable and churchwardens, who were enjoined to provide a book to keep their account in. Children caught begging were put to service.

By 1547 vagrancy had so greatly increased, due in part to the suppression of the monasteries, that an act, 1 Edw. VI., cap. 3, was passed, by which sturdy beggars were to be branded with the letter V, judged to be slaves for two years and compelled to do work, however vile—if need be, beaten, chained, or otherwise forced to comply. If he or she ran away, the fugitive when taken was branded with an S. Any child between the ages of 5 and 14 could be taken from its parents or legal guardians, with or without their consent, and put to work until 20 years of age ; if they ran away they might be sold into slavery.

Any conspiracy to damage their owner was met by a death penalty.

By the act of 1562-3 (5 Elizabeth, cap. 3) compulsory payments towards the support of the poor were for the first time ordered ; refusal to pay might mean imprisonment, but only after exhortation by the churchwardens and parson, and, this failing, the bishop.   If all these failed to untie the purse strings, the matter was reported to the justices, who then tried peaceable persuasion before bringing on the heads of recalcitrants the full penalty of the law.

This does not seem to have met the case, for the new act of 1572-3, 14 Elizabeth, cap. 5, re-enacted punishment by whipping and added burning through the ear.   Poor, aged, and impotent persons were to be provided for, and have convenient abiding places so that none need to wander.   Overseers of the poor were to be appointed and parishioners taxed to provide the necessary funds.

In the act of 18 Eliz., cap. 4, mothers of bastard children were ordered punishment, and the reputed father compelled to pay a certain fixed sum weekly, under pain of imprisonment.   This act is the basis of our subsequent bastardy laws.   Moreover, youths were to be trained to work and raw material provided for their instruction, houses of correction were appointed to deal with the unruly, persons wandering from their parishes to loiter and beg were whipped and sent back again.   It was hoped that by these means the provision of work and assured subsistence would check a public menace.

Under the act of the 39th of Elizabeth, cap. 3, churchwardens became *ex officio* overseers, and were assisted by four others appointed by the justices of the peace and the local Easter vestry.   They were empowered to set children to work and maintain them.   They could also raise necessary sums for the relief of the lame, impotent, old and blind ; apprentice poor children, and keep, of course, accounts of their expenditure.   It was followed up by an act of the same year cited as cap. 4; incorrigible rogues were stripped, whipped, and forwarded to their place of birth, or failing this sent to gaol.

Compulsory relief was fully and finally established by the act of 43 Elizabeth, cap. 2 (1600-1).

It is not necessary to follow in detail the various provisions made for the efficient tackling of the eternal problem of the unfit. Overseers' accounts, where they may be had, will throw a flood of light on the local working of the acts.

Sir Matthew Hales wrote a treatise in 1693 entitled "A Provision for the Poor," in which the system of workhouses is for the first time advocated—a system established two years later by the act quoted as 14 Charles II., cap. 12. Books were therein ordered to be procured and the names of all in receipt of parish relief set down, together with the causes why they had become liable to the benefit. This was wisely done to prevent the misuse of their new powers by the officials and serve as a check on the needless waste of the ratepayers' money.

By 1703 a few workhouses appeared sporadically in Worcestershire and elsewhere, built and conducted on similar lines to those of more recent date, but they were not definitely ordered until the act of 9 George I., cap. 7 (1722), when churchwardens and overseers were empowered to hire or purchase a house or houses, and to contract for lodging, maintaining and providing for the poor. Houses acquired under this act are still to be found and are a matter of some interest to the local historian. The union workhouses are of much later date and are still with us under another title. Whether or no it was kind and wise to take old folk from their lifelong habitats may well be doubted ; it was no doubt cheaper.

CHAPTER XIX.

CHILDREN OF THE VILLAGE.

The lot of the English peasant has ever been one of toil, his wife's was no better, and their offspring had an equally hard time. At a very early age they were made to be helpful to their parents, and even to-day in London one sees mites of girls with laden perambulators and small boys weighted down with firewood. In old days few thought any education necessary, though there was more of it, of good quality, than appears on the surface. In the Middle Ages the curriculum at the most embraced nothing more than the contents of the horn book, and consisted of religious instruction, viz., grace before and after meat, the " Creed, the Lord's Prayer, and the Ten Commandments in the vulgar tongue." Still, there were stirrings of some better thing, and in this matter Warwick-shire can hold its head proudly aloft with the best. The school in Warwick existing in the days of St. Edward the Confessor, within the precinct of the ancient monastery of All Saints, was even then reputed to have been held from time to which the memory of man extends not. This school, with all other its lands and privileges, was transferred to the Norman foundation of St. Mary's by Earl Roger in 1123 or soon after, but Henry I. seems to have re-transferred it in the same year. From that remote day to this it has played its part in the education of the youth of the town.

The statutes are in the chartulary of St. Mary's in the Public Record Office, and from this MS. we learn that the school had two "sides." The master of Grammar taught the Classics, the art of argument, philosophy, and rhetoric (the art of persuasion), which included composition, while the master of Song taught the young their letters, reading and writing, and music—a course not to be despised. If the chartulary is an example of their penmanship its result can be highly praised.

There was a similar school at Coventry as early as 1303 under the watchful eye of the monastery, and afterwards under the Cathedral body, but it was a secular school held in the city, taught by a secular master, and to it the boys of the town went to learn their grammar and take the thrashings so generously given as a stimulant to learning.

Nor was the Bishop's huge manor of Stratford behindhand. There too the flame of enlightenment was kindled. As early as 1295 a *rector scolarum* was ordained for the work of a teacher in this place, and by 1401 the Guild of the Holy Cross was providing one John Scolemayster with a chamber, and in 1426-7 the new schoolhouse was erected and has continued in use to the present day. The school and chapel were consecrated by the Bishop of the diocese, when a mighty feast was held. The Bishop's master cook, with two others of his household, four more from the town, and their assistants prepared the swans, herons, venison and other good fare for the rejoicing burgesses and guild brethren.

At a later date other schools arose as the great landowners began to realize their responsibilities. Thus, in 1635 a school was founded at Hampton Lucy owing to the munificence of the Rector, the Rev. Richard Hill; at Salford Priors William Perkins endowed a school in 1656, and quite a number of elementary schools arose before 1750. Alcester was founded by Walter Newport in 1582, Henley in Arden in 1586, Combrok by Sir Grevill Verney in 1641, Nuneaton in 1712, although there had been a grammar school here from 1552, at which a famous "barring out took place." The school was singularly unfortunate, and a long quarrel between the trustees and the master serves to throw a lurid light on the disciplinary methods of the day. One can only hope the Nuneaton master was exceptional.

A witness deposed that one John Wright had been whipped "until the blood dropped down from his tayle to his shoes, and hee was so sore that he could neither sit nor lye in his bed and was not well for a fortnight."

"This master, one Trevis, was charged with whipping boys, so that they were fain to pull the twigs out of their britch," and with bumping their heads upon their desks. This amiable imparter of knowledge was in the habit of getting very drunk, which in some sort explains matters, and something may be allowed for exaggeration.*

It is very much the fashion nowadays to forget the past, but the sincere thanks of the nation should go out to the multitude of very simple, very ignorant and yet conscientious teachers, who in the late eighteenth and early nineteenth centuries gave some sort of instruction to the villagers' children in "reading, 'riting and 'rithmetic," and above all the good manners that enabled them in other spheres to advance to good estate in life.

The aged Rector of one such school told the writer that the best mistress they ever had could neither read nor write, but all her pupils turned out well ; it may be that after all there is something beyond actual book learning carefully crammed into a college course.

Children found some time, in spite of work and school hours, to play games, and many of these are all but world-wide, witnessing their enormous antiquity. They are childish imitations of grown-ups and often show glimpses of ancient tribal feuds and friendships, but those who wish to do so can read Mrs. Gommes' splendid book, and learn from it what there is to be gathered.

There are, however, a few which seem to be rather local, and these ought to find a place here :—

Put.—This was played with a die which was rather oblong than a true cube. There was a pool to which each player paid a marble. The die—the "put"—was tossed up by the boys in turn; on its four sides were the letters P, T, H, L, and on its two ends A and D. If the "put" fell with the P side uppermost the thrower had to pay a marble to the pool, if with the T he took one, if with the H he was entitled to half the pool; the L was "let 'em alone" and a blank; A meant all, and the lucky player cleared the pool; but D implied that the thrower had to double the number in the pool. (F. S. P.)

Blind Egg.—Boys collect as many wild birds' eggs as possible and place them in a row. Then each boy is blindfolded in turn at a certain number of paces from the eggs, and advancing with a stick smashes as many of the eggs as he can in an allowed number of strokes.

Or as otherwise given—

Since there can be no luck in birds' nesting unless all eggs of a previous year have been destroyed, a game by which they may be broken in proper form has been provided. The string of eggs is laid on the ground and the boys form in line at a distance of some yards. One at a time, and closing both eyes, they hop in the direction of the eggs. Sometimes a breakage occurs, sometimes not; but the game goes on till all the eggs are broken. He that breaks most is supposed to be winner.

Conquers.—In this district the game of conquers was played with snail shells of the yellow or striped species. Two boys pressed the points of their respective snail shells together, and that which proved hardest and broke the other was conqueror. But if the losing shell had already broken others, they counted to its credit. A "conquer" of unusual strength might thus count some hundreds to its score.

Scobey Hunting.—This sport was known here as "Shackey-hunting," but was more practised in winter than summer. Boys filled their pockets with stones, and two or more went on the two sides of a hedge. Not unfrequently a bird would become so much confused by the stones hurled at it from different quarters as to be taken.

Lastly, Nine-Men's-Morris or its variants, five or three,

must be mentioned, since it was played in the meadow land of Whitchurch and elsewhere in the ancient and approved fashion till within living memory. Brand says it was "common among shepherds' boys in Warwick-shire," and played on the green turf or bare ground, the lines being cut or scratched to represent a species of chess-board, a square varying in size from a foot to three yards or more, within which is a smaller square with its sides parallel to the larger, and joined to it by diagonal lines connecting the angles and straight lines connecting the middle of sides. One party plays with wooden pegs, the other with stones, with which they devise the capture of each other's men, and those captured are placed in the inner square or pound. The green turf of the leys and the grass headlands were generally chosen. The full number of players was 18, 9 on each side.*

* Br. ii., p. 430.

CHAPTER XX.

A MEDLEY.

In this last chapter various odds and ends have been collected that would have otherwise escaped attention, some of them new and others old, but added in order to make the present work as far as possible complete.

Weather plays no unimportant part in the work and play of the countryside. Weatherwise villagers keep a watchful eye on its signs, especially in a district liable to floods, the sudden rising of a small stream such as the Stour causing danger by no means slight to any flocks left on the low-lying meadows. This river in an hour or so will overflow to the width of half a mile in places, and the frightened animals once caught by it are lost.

Ragged scuds of cloud running swiftly across the sky from the south-west are called " Severn Jacks," and considered a sign of heavy rain. Further on in the Vale of Evesham one hears—

> When Bredon Hill doth wear a cap,
> Men of the Vale beware a clap.

Nearer home—

> If Meon Hill be all mist and smoke
> Men of Crimscot look for a stroke.

There is a rhyme current foretelling a mild winter—

> If the Ice in October bear a Duck
> The rest of the year is all slush and muck.

Much of the land round Stratford-upon-Avon is either " tumbled down," in which case the thorn bushes on the grass balks have been allowed to spread at their

L

own sweet will until many hundreds of acres, once good barley ground, is now fit for rabbits only; or beautiful park lands and game-stocked coverts. Now where pheasants abound there poachers abound also. There has ever been a few adventurous souls who loved a scrap with a keeper, and dared to break forest law. Game-keepers had to deal with some rough customers in their time, and both sides were armed with *montels*. This weapon consisted of a short ashen staff to which an oval of boxwood was made fast by a leathern strap; this gave the moveable end sufficient play to make a very severe blow—if it fell on a man's head it might well be serious. A far more deadly instrument was in use in Whitchurch, where a noted poacher had a montel in which, in place of a wooden knob, the butt of a deer's antler filled with lead was attached; a stroke with this on the head of a gamekeeper must have caused death.

Trapping was formerly much in favour with the keeper; nowadays he is no longer allowed the cruel pole trap, but the writer has seen it in use. The trap itself was circular, laid on the flat top of a post set in the clearing of a wood and fixed by a chain. Bait was placed in the trap, and some hungry hawk or owl would swoop down and become caught by the feet in the jaws of the trap, and hang fluttering in agony until the keeper chanced to come that way or death put an end to its sufferings.

It is not so long ago that spring guns and man traps were in request to keep would-be trespassers from the preserves; a notice of the fact was conspicuously affixed to a tree. The charge in the gun was exploded by the trespasser catching a foot in a wire; it was not a pleasant experience.

Every village had at one time its stocks and pound; an example of the former still stands at Haselor, and those of Loxley and Ilmington exist or did so until recently. Mrs. Gaden of Preston-upon-Stour well remembers seeing a man in the stocks.

Hanging in effigy is twice recorded from Ilmington. In the one case the gallows was a poplar tree which grew on the church-land called Crow-yard at the lower end of the village green. This inscription was affixed:—

> This old bloke to Warwick went,
> False witness for to be,
> James Blomfield Rush
> Was for murder hung,
> This man for perjury.

After suspension for a while the effigy was cut down and burnt. The other case was that of a man named Wheatley, who rendered himself unpopular by enclosing part of the common land, the part of the green on which the stocks stood.

Since Chapter XVI. was set up there has come to light, among other forgotten notes, the words of the carol which follows. It was sung in the village of Armscote by an old lady named Plum, at that time 85 years of age. It is specially interesting since it contains two Saxon words, sensis and throstened.

King Herod and the Cock.

> There was a Star in David's land
>   Did in David's land appear,
> And in King Herod's chamber
>   So bright it did shine there.

> The Wise Men they soon spied it
>   And told the King on high
> That a Prince's Babe was born that night
>   No King should e'er destroy.

> If this be the truth, King Herod said,
>   That thou hast told to me,
> The Roasted Cock that lies in the dish
>   Shall crow full " sensis " three.

> Oh, the Cock soon "throstened" and feathered well
>   By the works of God's own hand,
> And he did crow full sensis three
>   In the dish where he did stand.

A few notes on the flowers, wild and cultivated, that have attracted the notice of our folk should be given a place, though there is little new to be said about them.

Of the flowers of Springtide the Narcissus is known
as all its tribe by the pretty name of " Sweet Nancies."
It used to be the custom, a modern one of course, of
going a-primroseing in Lark Stoke woods to gather
" pale Primroses " for the church decoration on Easter
Day.   The closely related Cowslip was much in request,
and many women made a small harvest collecting the
flower heads and drying them for cowslip wine.   These
" pips," as the dried flowers were called, had a ready sale
locally.

Many flowers bear the name of Cuckoo-flower, among
them the Lady's Smock, one of the flowers dedicated to
the Blessed Virgin Mary, mentioned upon page 125, but
Lady's Laces and Lady's Signet were accidentally omitted.
The Cuckoo-flower mentioned in King Lear is the wild
Geranium, either the cut-leaved or the soft-leaved.   This
name is well known in the Stratford district.   Cuckoo-
buds may be the Marsh Marygold, to which the ugly
name of Horse Blobbs is now very generally given.

All blue flowers are Devil's flowers and unlucky,
especially the Germander Speedwell.   In the gardens that
old world favourite the Love-in-the-Mist is also called
Devil-in-a-bush ; the flower is, of course, a blue colour.
Elder, as the tree on which Judas hung himself, should
never be used as firing ; not only does the Devil sit on
the chimney but the fire will not burn.   Yet its flowers
are used for the complexion, steeped in water.   " Bache-
lor's Buttons " is the local name for the White Campion,
Gilliflowers are Wallflowers, Whitsun Gillies the Dame's
Violet, Honeysuckle is locally known as Wide-wind, the
Small Bindweed as Way-wind.

Flax played an important part in old days, since linen
thread was a necessity.   There are orders in the court
rolls against " watering flax in the Stower."   The garden
Pansy is still called Love-in-idleness or Kiss-me-over-the-
garden-gate.   This little plant has acquired such popularity that it has a long list of local names, a pretty good
sign of affection on the part of the people.

Bryony roots are called Mandrakes, and are still in

request. The genuine root was probably quite unknown in the country.

The common Marygold (*Calendula officinalis*) has of late years regained much of its old-time popularity. It is yet another of the many flowers dedicated to the Virgin Mary, as its old name "Seynte Marie Rode" shows. It was used in the kitchen to colour cheese and also a favourite at funerals. The Shakesperian name for Clover, Honey-stalks, is not forgotten at Whitchurch, where Mr. John Mayo spoke of it under that name. This is one of the "finds" an enthusiastic searcher likes to run across. He certainly had not read the play.

This chapter may well conclude with a characteristic letter to the author from Mr. Potter, which shows how his knowledge and critical faculty assisted in the preparation of the manuscript.

Halford, S.-on-S.

15 Feb. 1915.

Dear Mr. Bloom,

Rosemary is not an abundant herb even now, and when we consider its property of growing only in those gardens where the mistress is master, it must have been still more rare in former times. Hence the necessity of sometimes finding a substitute for it, and why not broom?

I take the custom of the bride first putting a knife into the cake to be one of genuine native antiquity, and not like Christmas-trees and golden weddings, a mere modern importation from Germany.

I have sought in vain among my 17 c. receipt-books for some formula for making Caudle. Ale, and sometimes I think wine, but never I believe water, was used. Caudle wells abound—there is one at Shipston and one at Tredington—but I have always looked upon the name as a mispronunciation of "cold-well." Its modern form would naturally incline the village folk to connect it with "caudle."

If the gipsies really did jump a broomstick by way of marriage ceremony we have a plausible explanation of the common phrase. But brooms were not much in evidence in gipsy life, unless among those who were in the besom trade. Are you aware that it was a tradition in this district that if a man hung out a broom in front of his house, it was to be taken as an intimation that he was in want of a housekeeper or female companion of some sort? I can recall one instance in which it was done, at Hidcote Boise. Could this custom have any connection with the phrase in question?

I have no acquaintance with the necklaces you mention, but I know that there is among our village women a prejudice in favour of hanging necklaces of some kind round the necks of young children, the motive being some vague idea of its bringing "luck" to the child rather than as ornament.

I was aware that some anointing of the newly-born was practised, but supposed to be rather for protection of the tender skin than as ceremonial. But what is your explanation of the following :—

I have been told by my mother that in my earliest days I did not thrive as a well-conducted baby ought to have done, on which my wise old nurse pronounced that the brains of a hare must be given me. As I had been born at Midsummer when hares are not in season some difficulty arose. However, the hare was caught and the brains duly administered, after which I suppose I mended my manners.

I have this morning some ancient British coins. They are uninscribed and not quite satisfactory. I am not sure that I shall keep them.

With kind regards,

Sincerely yours,

F. SCARLETT POTTER.

APPENDIX I.

A Legend of Long Compton.

From the *Historia Aurea* of John Tinemuth.

"About the year of our Saviour's Incarnation, Dciiii, St. Augustine, being arrived in England to preach the Gospell, came hither; whereupon the Priest of the Parish repaired to him and made a complaint that the Lord of the Town, not paying his Tithes, although admonished, was by him excommunicated, and yet stood more obstinate. St. Augustine therefore, conventing him for that fault, demanded the reason of such his refusall. 'Knowest thou not' (quoth he) 'that they are not thine, but God's?' To whom the Knight answered, 'Did not I plow and sow the land; I will therefore have the tenth sheaf as well as the nine.' Whereupon St. Augustine replyed, 'If thou will not pay them I will excommunicate thee,' and so hastning to the Altar publickly said, 'I command that no excommunicate person be present at Masse,' which words were no sooner spoke than that a dead man that lay buried at the entrance into the church immediately arose out of his Grave, went without the compass of the Churchyard, and there stood during the time of Mass, which being finished St. Augustine went to him and said, 'I command thee, in the name of God, that thou tell me who thou art.' To whom he made answer, 'I was Patron of this Place in the time of the Britains, and though frequently warned by the Priest, yet never would I pay him my Tithes, and so dyed excommunicate, and was thrust into Hell.' Which answer occasioned St. Augustine to command him to shew where the Priest was buried that so excommunicated him, who, being directed to his Grave, said, 'To the end that all men may know that life and death are in the hands of God, to whom nothing is impossible, Arise in his name, for we have need of thee.' Who thereupon

came out of his Grave and stood before them.   To whom
St. Augustine said, 'Brother, dost thou know this man?'
'Yes,' quoth he, 'but I would 1 had never known him,
for he was alwaies a Rebell to the church, a witholder of
his Tithes, and even to his last a very wicked man, which
occasioned me to excommunicate him.'

   " St. Augustine replyed, 'Brother, thou knowest that
God is mercifull, therefore we must have pity on this
miserable creature, who is the image of God, and
redeem'd with his bloud, having so long endured the
pains of Hell.'   Wherefore, delivering to him a scourge,
he kneeled down, and craving absolution with tears, had
it granted ; and so by St. Augustine's command, returning to his grave again, was immediately resolved to dust.
Then said St. Augustine to the Priest, 'How long hast
thou been buried?'   'Above an hundred and fifty years,'
quoth he.   *Aug.*, 'How hast thou fared hitherto?'
'Well,' quoth the Priest, 'enjoying the delights of eternal
life.'   *Aug.*, 'Art thou contented that I should pray unto
God that thou may'st return again to us, and by thy
preaching reduce many souls unto him that are deceived
by the Devill?'   'Far be it from thee, O Father,' quoth
the Priest, 'that thou shouldest disturb my quiet as to
bring me back to the troublesome life of this world.'
Aug., 'Go thy way then and rest in peace, praying for
me and for the Universall Church of God' : so accordingly entring his grave he fell also to dust.   Then turn'd
St. Augustine to the Knight and said, 'Wilt thou now
pay thy Tithes to God my son?'   Who trembling and
weeping fell at his feet, and, confessing his offence, craved
pardon, and, shaving himself, became a follower of
St. Augustine all the days of his life."

                    Dugdale (ed. Thomas), i. 581.

APPENDIX II.

GUY OF WARWICK, AND COLBRAN.

"In the year 926 the Danes invaded and cruelly wasted England, reaching almost to Winchester. It was eventually agreed that champions should be chosen for either host, and the Danes promised that if their man lost they would leave the land. This Danish warrior was named Colbran. Athelstan enjoyned a fast of 3 days and prayed for aid. 'God being moved .... sent a good angell to comfort the King as he lay upon his bed, the very night of the Nativity of St. John Bapt., directing that he should arise early on the morrow, taking two Bishops with him, and get up to the North gate of the City, staying there till the hour of Prime, and then should he see .... a personable man in a Pilgrim's habit, barefooted, with his head uncovered and upon it a chaplet of white Roses ; and that he should intreat him, for the love of Jesu Christ, the devotion of his Pilgrimage and the preservation of all England, to undertake the Combat.' Athelstan, with the Archbishop of Canterbury and the Bishop of Chichester, did as he was warned to do. Thus did the King meet with Guy, who had hastened to Winchester in view of the terrible state of the Kingdom. The King fully explained the danger of the situation, Guy meanwhile dissembling his real name, and after three weeks' repining rose on the appointed day, heard three masses—of the Holy Ghost, the second of the Holy Trinity, the 3rd of the Holy Cross, and thus prepared, mounted the King's best charger, and armed with lance and the Sword of the great Constantine, set out for the valley called Chiltecumbe, where he awaited the giant Colbrand. The fight lasted all day, but at even the Dane was despatched."

Dugdale, i. 374.

APPENDIX III.

Specimen of the Services due from a Villain on the Manor of Old Stratford in 1252.

CUSTOMARY (TENANTS) OF SOTHRIE.

Simon Bithebroke holds a messuage and a virgate of land at 8*s.* per annum, payable at the four terms, and owes Warselver on St. Martin, and toll for each horse born to him, should it be sold within the manor, 1*d.*, and for an ox . . . . and for a pig over a year old 1*d.*, and of less age ½*d.*, but it may not be a sucking pig. And he cannot sell pork from the Feast of St. Peter in chains to that of St. Andrew without leave of the lord. He owes help at the ale-making of the lord, that is called *fulfthale*, and at the ale-making for the lord's cellar, and shall give one silver penny for himself and his wife. He owes toll of ale, when he shall brew for sale, 1*d.*, and owes help at the Feast of St. Michael and hundred selver, and owes heriot at his death, viz., the best animal that he shall have. He owes prison guard in his turn and to lead to Warewike. He is not able to send away his son, nor to marry his daughter without his lord's leave, and they (the jury) say that his full rate is 8*s.*, and that he does no work at any time.

And when he has been at work for all the year then he will be quit of 5*s.* and 1*d.*, and owes at the Feast of St. Andrew 11*d.*, at the Feast of the Blessed Mary in March 11*d.*, and at the Nativity of St. John the Baptist 12*d.*, and he shall work every week from the Feast of St. Michael the Arch to the Feast of St. Andrew for one day, viz., to plough and to harrow, to hoe and to reap, or what else he may be ordered at the will of his lord, and in the same manner from the Feast of St. Andrew until the Feast of St. John. And from the Feast of St. John until the Feast of St. Michael he shall work every week four days with one man, and at the time of harvest (Messis) every week he shall come with one man to Bederipp (reaping) of the lord until the corn of the lord shall be gathered in. In the meanwhile, if his own corn be harvested before that of his lord, he owes it with one man or two at his lord's will, to collect his lord's corn assiduously until all shall be collected. And he owes it to cart hay or corn from any virgate as often as the work shall be required. And it shall be reckoned for his work. And he owes in like manner horse labour for his work as often as it shall be done, and none the less he owes all customs and toll of pannage to redeem his sons and daughters, and his work and customary services are reckoned for the year at 9s. 8d., and in the meanwhile he owes a strike and a half of corn of chersett (tithe corn) at St. Martin.

APPENDIX IV.

Specimen of the Will of a rich Warwickshire Yeoman.

In Dei nomine Amen. The xxviii[th] day of September In the yere of our Lord god a thousande fyve hundred twenty and sevynne, I Richard Buller of longe Comptone, seke in body hole of mynde and remembraunce, make my testament in this maner of wise hereafter folowing. First I bequethe my soule to Almightye god to our Lady Saint Mary and to all the Company of hevynne and my body to be buried in the Churche Yarde of long Comptone. Also I bequeathe to the Mother Churche of Worcetor vid. To the high awter of long Comptone vid. and to the Sacrament of the said awter to have a clothe of silke iijs. iiijd. To Saint Austen of the same to have a taper to be maintayned for my fader and me the space of foure yeres price xxd. To the Sepulture light iijs. iiijd. To Our Lady light, to Saint Katherine lighte, to Saint Nicolas, to Saint Clement, to Saint

George, to the Rode everiche of these a shepe. To the
belles iiij shepe.   To the Lampe light iiij*d*.   Item to the
church of Long Comptone a cope price iiij marks.   To
the Chapel in Westone for my fader and me xx*s*.   Item
I bequethe to have a prest to serve in Comptone Churche
for my fader and moder and me with all my goode
frendes oon yere viii marces.   Item I bequethe to
Cheryngton Churche, to Stowreton Chapell, to Wolford
Chapell, everych of them a calfe of a yere age.   Item
I bequeth to Sir James White x*s*., to Sr Richard Warde
iij*s*. iiij*d*.   Item I bequethe to Agnes my wife xvi store
shepe and viii score of them to be wynteryde at Westone.
Item I bequethe to Agnes my wife vi oxen, xii kyne,
xii yong beastes, vii horses and mares, my best cart with
the harneyse longing therto, a paire of wollen wheles,
and all the corne longing to the parsonage bothe tithe and
glebe, and the money that Thomas Robynes oweth me
for tithe Corne the sume of vi*li*. x*s*. iiij*d*. and vii quarters
of whete, and alle the housholde stuffe that she had
before I maried her, and the encrease of my duffe house
in Westone this oon yere, and all my olde malt except two
quarters, and to Mawde her daughtere a kowe.   Item
I bequethe to my brother John Buller fyve score shepe,
iiij oxen, oon heiffer, two quarters of whete and two
quarters of malt and the money that Henry Derande of
Worcetur oweth me whiche is x*s*.   Item I bequethe to
Thomas Joyner thre score shepe, a horse, a mare, two
oxen and half a quarter of whete, a yok, a cowe.   Item
to William his brother fiftye shepe, two oxene, a horse,
a mare, a yock, a cowe, half a quarter of whete, and the
said Thomas and William to have between them a matres,
a paier of shetes and a coverlet, a cart tyre and x*s*. to bye
them wheles and nayles.   Item to Richard Prewe and
Robert Prewe either of them 40 shepe and either of them
a heiffer.   Item I bequethe to Agnes my doughtere a
fetherbed, ij paire of shetes, and a shete with a blake seme,
xij pewter disshes, a pair of beads that were hir moders,
fyve hundred shepe and xl beasts.   To Dorathe my
doughter a fetherbed, ij paire of shetes, ffyve hundred

shepe and xl beasts. And the said Agnes and Dorathe
to have betweene them vi silver spones. Item to George
Osbaston my beste graye colt of ij yeres olde. Item to
Richard Wilkynes a colt price vis. viiid. Item to John
Byg a heiffer. Item to Robert Franklen a mare. Item
to John Buller of Sutton a mare. Item to Yong Thomas
Hidon of Wolforde a bullock of ij yeres old. Item to
Colettes wifes dowghter of Sutton xx sheep and two
kowe calves, and these xx shepe and ij calves to be kept
in my grounde at Weston during the yeres of my takyng
for the sight of my executors. The residue of my goodes
not bequethed after my body be buried, my debtes paid,
and my legacies fulfilled I give and bequeathe to Agnes
and Dorathe my doughters, and they to have Weston
with all commodities longing therto during the yeres of
my taking to kepe their catall uppon. And the said
Agnes and Dorathe my doughters with their goodes and
catall and with thencreasement thereof to be in the
guyding and gouernance of John Busby of Burmyngton
till they be of lawfull age, and if oon of these children
dye the other childe to have hir parte with hir owne
parte. And if both these childrene dye I will that my
brother John Buller and his childrene have xxli. of the
forsaid goodes. And Cherington Churche to have v
marces and the residue of my goodes to mortize a priest
to serve in Longe Compton church yf they will extende
thereto, yf not I will that they be bestowed for the welthe
of my soule and my goode frendes as my executores and
overseeres thinke best. And to this my testament I ordeyn
and make John Busbye of Burmyngton and John Buller
of Sutton my executoures to perfourme and fulfill my
wille above writene. And these foresaid executoures to
paye almaner of Dues longing to the children withe the
childrenes goodes and they executoures to have yerely
till the children be of lawful age either of them xxs., and
as ofte as these executores Ride or goe in busyness
longing to my testament or to my childrene I will that they
alowe them selfes conciently for their labour and costes
of the foresaide childeren goodes. And also I ordeyn and

make Syr James White, my brother John Buller, Richard Wilkynes, and John Byg overseers, that my will be perfourmed and fulfilled as is abovewritten. Proved at London 8 Nov. 1527. (P.C.C., 25, Porch.)

APPENDIX V.

GUY OF WARWICK.

The legend of the Dun Cow is unknown before the mention of it by Dr. Caius in his book *De Rariorum Animalium Historia Libellus*, printed in London in the year 1570. He writes :—

"I met with the head of a certain huge animal, of which the naked bone, with the bones supporting the horns, were of enormous weight, and as much as a man could well lift . . . . Of this kind I saw another head at Warwick in the castle A.D. 1552. There is also the vertebra of the neck of the same animal, of such great size that its circumference is not less than three Roman feet seven inches and a half. I think also that the blade-bone which is to be seen hung up in chains from the North gate of Coventry belongs to the same animal. In the chapel of the great Guy, Earl of Warwick . . . . at Guys Cliff there is hung up a rib of the same animal . . . . Some of the common people fancy it to be the rib of a wild boar killed by Sir Guy, some the rib of a cow which haunted a ditch near Coventry and injured many persons. The last I take it to be nearer the truth, since it may perhaps be the bone of Bonasus or Urus."

It is thus alluded to in "The Tragical History and Admirable Achievements of Guy, Earl of Warwick," written by J. B. London, 1661.

.... and now again
He combats with that huge and monstrous beast
Called the wild Cow of Dunsmore Heath.

And in another place—

And by thy hand the wild Cow slaughtered
That kept such revels upon Dunsmore Heath.

An eighteenth century chap book tells the story thus :—

"On the return of Guy from abroad he heard the report about the Country of a monstrous Cow which terrified the neighbouring places, destroying the Cattle, and hurting and killing many that went about to destroy her ; she was beyond the ordinary size of other Cattle, six yards in length and four high, with large sharpe horns and fiery eyes of a Dun Colour ; her place of abode was on a Heath near Warwick, now called Dunsmore Heath, which derives its name from this Monstrous Cow. The King, hearing of the dreadful havock this Beast made, offered Knighthood to any that should overcome this Dun Cow. Guy, who was thought to be far beyond the Sea, privately arming himself with a strong Battleaxe and his Bow and Quiver, made his way towards the Place where this Monster was, and approaching near the Den he beheld upon the Heath the sad objects of Desolation, the Carcases of Men and Beasts she had destroyed. Guy, no whit daunted at that, pursued on his way, till such time she espied Guy, staring with her dreadful eyes at him and roaring most hideously ; he bent his bow of steel and let fly an arrow, which rebounded from her hide as if it had been shot against a Brazen Wall ; she, enraged, ran as swift as the Wind at him, who, seeing his Arrows of no effect, had prepared with his Battle Axe to receive her, which he did with such a Blow upon her head as made her recoil, but she recovering, more enraged at such Treatment, ran full tilt with her Sharp Horns at Guy's Breast, which only dented his Armour and made

him stagger ; laying on many Blows, at last he hit her
under the Ear, which was the only Place that was
penetrable, where, making a deep Wound, the Blood
gushed out amain, and he, following his Blows in the
same Place, made so many Gashes that with loud roaring
she fell down and, weltering in a stream of Blood, died."

APPENDIX VI.

ONE-HANDED BROUGHTON.

" In Lawford Hall, I am told, a room was preserved as
the bedchamber of an ancestor of the family, who, in the
time of Elizabeth, having lost an arm, went afterwards
by the appellation of One-handed Broughton.   After his
death the room was reported to be haunted, and as such
many attempts were made to sleep in, but in vain, ...
it was with difficulty any labourer could be prevailed on
to assist in pulling it down.   The ghost . . . . had been
frequently seen . . . . riding across the neighbouring
grounds in a coach and six . . . . I was informed that his
perturbed spirit had been laid by a numerous body of the
clergy, who conjured it into a phial and threw it into a
marle pit opposite the house.

" John Wolf, who died a reputed centenarian, said :
' That twelve parsons met to lay the ghost, that the
candles of eleven of them went out, that Parson Hall's
candle remained burning, and that he laid the ghost, but
that it was to have a certain space of time every night in
which to wander abroad.' "

M. Bloxham, *Medieval Legends of*
Warwickshire, p. 12.

APPENDIX VII.

Wroth Silver.*

" At sunrise on Saturday Nov. 11 the Duke of Buc-cleuch, through the intermediary of his agent, observed at Knighton Hill the curious custom of collecting, as Lord of the Manor of the Hundred of Knightlow, 'Wroth Silver' or 'Wroth Penny' from various parishes in the Hundred. The ceremony, which it is believed dates from Saxon times, was witnessed by a large number of people from Coventry, Leamington, Dunchurch, Rugby and other places. On Saturday it commenced in the usual manner, the Duke's agent read the Charter of Assembly and then formally called upon the several parishes to make the payment. The amounts due vary from a penny to two shillings and threepence, and as the Wroth Silver is paid it is dropped into a hole in the stone of the Cross. All of the parishes 'called' on Saturday paid, with the exception of Long Itchington, and accord-ing to old custom the Duke of Buccleuch can impose for non-payment of these fees a fine of 20s. for every penny not forthcoming, or else the forfeiture of a white bull with a red nose and ears of the same colour.† This fine has been once enforced during the present century, a white bull having been demanded by the Steward of the late Lord John Scott, then Lord of the Hundred. After the ceremony at the Stone, the steward, following the usual custom, invited those who contributed to a very substantial breakfast at an inn in the village of Stretton-on-Dunsmore."

Notes and Queries, 8th Series, iv. 497,
Dec. 16, 1893.

---

* Wroth or Ward Silver is a payment in lieu of military service.
† The white bull, the extinct wild cattle of England.

APPENDIX VIII.

Place Names.

The following list of places and the derivation of their names is taken from Duignan's little book on this subject :—

Alcester (the fortress on the Alne), Alveston (Eanwulf's town), Aston (East town), Atherston upon Stour (Æthelric's town), Ayleston (Ælfurth's town), Bidford (the ford of Pudda), Binton (the town of the sons of Bynna), Birmingham (the house of the sons of Brme), Brailes (*unknown*, probably Celtic), Charlescot (the Ceorl's cot), Ruyne-Clifford (the rugged ford of the cliff), Clopton (Cloppa's town), Compton (Combe town), Crimscote (Coenhelm's cottage), Eatington (Ettings hill), Exhall (Ecles meadow), Halford (the ford of the meadow), Hampton (high town), Hunscot (Hunstan's cottage), Idlicote (Æthelyn's cottage), Ilmington (Eadhelm's town), Kineton (King's town), Luddington (Luda's town), Milcote (Mill cottage), Newbold (New house), Nuneaton (Nuns' town on running water), Oxhill (a shelf of sloping land), Pathlow (Peufa's moor), Preston (priests' town), Shottery (Scotta's meadow), Snitterfield (Sniter's field), Stratford (the ford on the street), Teddington (Tedda's town), Thelesford (Tæfles town), Tysoe (Tih's hill), Whatcote (Watta's cottage), Wimpston (Wilhelm's town), Wixford (Witlac's ford), Wolford (Wulweard's . . . ., ? *something now lost*), Wootton Wawen (Town in the wood).

INDEX

LONDON

THE ROMANCE OF ITS DEVELOPMENT

BY

GEO. E. EADES, M.A., F.S.A. Scot.

LECTURER IN LONDON HISTORY, L.C.C. CITY LITERARY INSTITUTE.

Price 7s. 6d. nett.

Press Opinions :—

" Something of the history of the whole of London area and of its people, including Greater London and the Metropolitan Boroughs. He ranges over the whole field from British to Modern London. . . . . His book should serve as a good introduction to larger works."—*The Times*, 16 September, 1927.

" . . . . an excellent book . . . . an exposition of the soul of London as it speaks to us in its stones and in its streets, in the accumulation of its memories and the pageantry of its evolution. Mr. Eades knows his London well and loves it. Not an aspect of its many-sided historical appeal is overlooked ; not a side-stream that finds its way shyly into the main current of development but is affectionately explored . . . . The narrative is punctuated with anecdotes and picturesque details showing us how the Londoners of past generations lived and worked and played."—*Evening Standard*, 16 September, 1927.

" . . . . our author . . . . tells briefly, brightly and informatively the story of London from the very earliest times to the present day. . . . . The chapter on Medieval London is singularly delightful. Mr. Eades gives a graphic description of London life at that time and of the conditions under which the people lived. . . . . We have seldom come across a more vivid picture of medieval London. . . . . Apart altogether from its interest the volume will prove very valuable in the direction of inspiring others . . . . to become conversant with the fascinating history of London."—*City Press*, 24 September, 1927.

" This very interesting volume . . . . presents a remarkably rich store of materials . . . . the term " romance " used in the title is entirely appropriate . . . . a valuable bibliography appended to the book is specially rich in references to local history . . . . the work is one to be studied . . . . by all to whom the present life of our people is a subject of the profoundest thought."—*Inquirer*.

Mitchell Hughes and Clarke, 11-13 Bream's Buildings, London, E.C. 4.